JORAM

Praise for *Joram*, a feature film based on two stories in this book

'... Bressonian tension ... sizzling action, lawless atmosphere and lively locations ... presented with undeniable vigour and detail.'

—Lou Thomas, *Sight And Sound*

'... reminds us what radical storytelling feels like... nuanced, gorgeously subdued ... a political drama about indigenous survival masked as a pulse-pounding crime thriller.'

—Rory Doherty, *Projektor*

'*Joram* isn't meant to be entertaining but it is gripping from start to finish ... first-rate performances that enhance the impact of the film ... an immersive and disturbing man-on-the-run drama ...'

—Saibal Chatterjee, *NDTV*

'Never have I seen themes of displacement and existential crisis being explored so beautifully on-screen.'

—Vijayalakshmi Narayanan, *Free Press Journal*

'…makes a striking impact.'

—Namrata Joshi, *Screen Daily*

'The women characters make a teleological break in how the genre has been presented and consumed over time … they keep the adrenaline high and pace intense while breaking the tropes and archetypes.'

—Tanushree Ghosh, *Moneycontrol*

'An intense and gripping genre film – a survival thriller … lets the social commentary simmer under the surface, not letting it overpower the tense atmosphere …"

—Virat Nehru, *High on Films*

'A thrilling film, beautifully shot, well acted, and an exciting manhunt mystery.'

—Ard Vijn, *Screen Anarchy*

'A fast-paced survival thriller.'

—Naman Ramachandran, *Variety*

'Haunting.'

—Devarsi Ghosh, *Mint*

'Where *Joram* excels, and what makes it stand apart, is that it is not primarily interested in its genre roots, or the manhunt, but instead the world in which it takes place and the bigger social issues that it tackles.'

—Anthony Frajman, *FilmInk Australia*

'An excellent movie… a wonder to look at.'

—Panos Kotzathanasis, *Asian Movie Pulse*

'*Joram* is in an incredible feat … Definitely a film I would not mind queuing up for an hour at a festival.'

—Kalpana Nair, *IMDB*

'An outstanding political thriller in the tradition of the 1970s Italian and French crime films, investigating government corruption and the ordinariness of evil in modern capitalist society.'

—International Film Festival, Rotterdam

'[An] edge-of-your-seat survival thriller that deftly weaves political intrigue with a stylish and propulsive cinematic sensibility … skillfully creates great tension while gradually revealing the political underpinnings of the thrilling action.'

—Sydney Film Festival

'Delivers intense genre filmmaking with heart-stopping moments of peril, while bringing piercing intelligence and empathy to the globally resonant struggles of indigenous people displaced.'

—Edinburgh International Film Festival

'The thriller is a race across India's troubled interior. You will be sitting on the edge of your seat, as the drama unfolds …'

—Durban International Film Festival

'Some of the very best action scenes of the year, including an incredibly choreographed chase scene where the lead character has a baby strapped to him the whole time. Really harrowing, nail-biting stuff!'

—Sam Flancher, *Chicago International Film Festival*

'... masterfully subverts cinematic conventions, blending thriller, noir, and western elements. Through a mesmerizing narrative that oscillates between heart-pounding pursuit and introspective exploration, *Joram* lays bare the desperation that can arise from societal inequalities, offering a powerful and unapologetic examination of the human condition in the face of adversity.'

—International Film Festival of South Asia, Toronto

'Fervor, rawness and edge ... Action-packed, sophisticated storytelling ... *Joram* invites us to reflect upon the moral implications of the hefty price of "progress".'

—Indian Film Festival of Los Angeles

'*Joram* is a heart-thumping survival thriller with a hard political edge.'

—*London Indian Film Festival*

JORAM

DEVASHISH MAKHIJA

HarperCollins *Publishers* India

First published in India as *Forgetting*
by HarperCollins *Publishers* India 2014
4th Floor, Tower A, Building No. 10, Phase II, DLF Cyber City,
Gurugram, Haryana – 122002
www.harpercollins.co.in

2 4 6 8 10 9 7 5 3 1

This edition published by HarperCollins *Publishers* 2024

Illustrations by Devashish Makhija

P-ISBN: 978-93-6213-512-4
E-ISBN: 978-93-6213-379-3

Typeset in 10.5/14.5 Electra LT Std at
R. Ajith Kumar

Printed and bound at
Replika Press Pvt. Ltd.

MIX
Paper | Supporting responsible forestry
FSC™ C016779
FSC www.fsc.org

This book is produced from independently certified FSC® paper to ensure responsible forest management.

In these pages, a few people from my life whom I have loved and been loved by, both intensely, are sure to recognize themselves. All, except for my mother, Bharati Makhija, who will never read this book. But who, by passing, somehow bequeathed it to me. *Forgetting* (*Joram*) is for her, because it can't be.

CONTENTS

'It's difficult to judge the distance of the past. It could be an inch or ten miles away from remembering. From the moment something happens to the point it becomes memory, is monumentally immeasurable.'

—Ted Mckeever (Meta4)

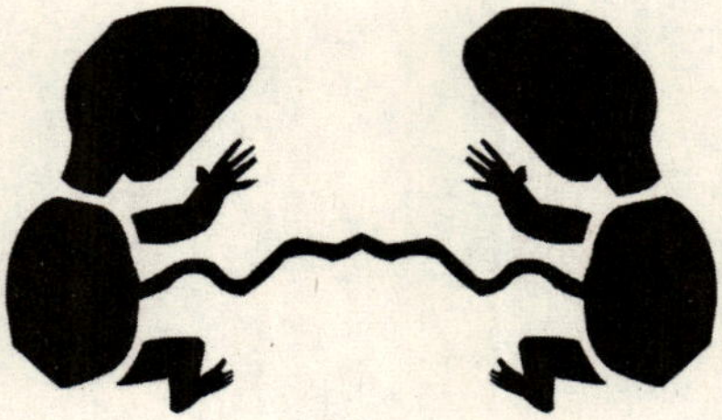

BY/TWO

1. Rahim

He liked the night shift, thought Rahim, tilting his head back and filling his lungs with the black sooty sky, as his bladder quickly emptied below. He could piss into the sea, even spit his paan into it, and no one would mind. Because at night, Mumbai was a tired, brutalized, hurting, heaving whore. She didn't give a fuck who pissed in her seas. It was only during the day that Mumbai creaked, crunched, rattled and rushed like a desperate machine.

And you dare not piss in a machine. It gets pissed off. And then it crunches your balls between its tooth-gear wheels.

Rahim remembered telling Rahman that over dinner one day, gesticulating so wildly that the dal chaawal sprayed out of his mouth, the same way that the shit had burst out of their rickshaw's exhaust pipe during the surprise PUC inspection. Rahman had looked at Rahim sternly and said, 'Don't talk that way, this city is our Mecca, it feeds you and me despite the lies we tell. Don't offend it. It could as well turn into our jehannum.'

Rahim tired of his brother's fear of hell. 'Take Langdi out at night once,' he'd gestured to Rahman, 'and you'll know. By daylight, even a murderer looks like he could do with a hug.' Rahman never took his advice. He grimaced each time Rahim referred to their autorickshaw as 'Langdi', the lame one. But Rahim needed to remind himself. What self-respecting man would ride a beast with three legs? A beast that doesn't gallop, but sneaks and swerves slyly to survive. A goonga perhaps would. A handicapped vehicle deserves a handicapped rider.

Langdi, like Rahim, was made to survive Mumbai. She was an old machine, the kind that had the engine in the front, one that wouldn't pull it up an incline, but one that vibrated like a drill machine. Rahim didn't mind the vibration. He didn't mind it so much that even when he was waiting for a passenger to show up he'd keep the engine running, enjoying the tremors running up the insides of his legs like a cheap champi tel massage. Also, Langdi had a large gassy behind, just like ammi's. If Rahim wasn't wrong, he had a feeling Rahman thought so too.

What a strange thought, mused Rahim, as he turned away from the oily edge of the Versova sea and plodded through the sodden sand, not caring to check if it were the masticated remnants of the evening high tide he stepped in or someone's pasty turds. In the darkness it's one and the same, he said to himself, and heaved his slight self over some rocks to get to the main road, where Langdi stood, her insides throbbing with a Himesh Reshammiya song. Rahim slid into the ghostly blue-lit interior of his rickshaw, turned down the music, grabbed the starting lever near his feet, jerked it upwards and made Langdi cough and shudder to life. That shudder always made Rahim hard. It reminded him of the way he shuddered in the sandaas some mornings when he grabbed and tugged at himself.

'Made up for the lack of rain out there, did you?' a voice

from the passenger seat barked at him. Rahim grinned into the rear-view mirror hanging out of the side of the windscreen the way a footboard traveller does out of an overcrowded BEST bus. 'Chhee, those teeth need a PUC test,' the voice squealed. Rahim now gesticulated into the mirror, 'Where to?' The woman in the back leaned out, the breeze whipping her powdered face, her small blouse battling to keep her breasts inside it, and mumbled 'Infiniti'.

The further out of the speeding auto Ramdulari swung, the further down the driver's seat Rahim slid, as if to maintain the precarious balance of the rickshaw, but in truth to keep her ample reflection from slipping out of the little round window of the rear-view mirror. She was his most consistent passenger. On good nights he made more money than Rahman made in a week. But he never let on how. Or Rahman would slap his own forehead so hard it would kick a 'Lahaulwillaquwat' out of his God-fearing lips. Jehannum, he would say, we'll go to jehannum for this.

Rahim hated to admit that Rahman was not entirely wrong.

They had come to Mumbai from Akbarpur, a small filth-heap of a town that sprang up along the railway tracks soon after the East India Company ran the first train across the nation's breasts. It was a town forever in transit, a quick-halt junction for mostly goods' trains. As a result all the businesses in Akbarpur centred around food, the only commodity people passing through really need. Their father was a kasaai, the butcher with the dirtiest mouth in the town square. So dirty, that he used to cuss his first wife even as he exploded inside her, cursing her for not being able to bear him any children. And then he cussed his second when she bore him not one, but two, simultaneously!

So dirty was his mouth that word was he never threw away the shit that came out of the intestines of the goats he cut open: he ate it all.

But Rahim knew better. Ever since he could walk, he used to be given that shit to dispose of, along with the tree stump abba used as a chopping block, each night, to clean it of all the little bits of rotting meat that clung to it. Rahim's childhood passed in a blur of bleating goats, morose cows and dead meat. Rahman however stayed hidden behind their mother's abundant girth. In the hefty shadows there he must have discovered the fear of God, thought Rahim often. Abba didn't dare inseminate their mother again for fear that she might bear triplets the next time around! Instead, he married a third time.

Most nights when Rahim would stand alone at the rim of the toilet bowl that was Akbarpur, and toss little bits of rotting meat up into the air for the eagles to grab and devour, he looked across the landscape, towards the west, and thought of the large sparkling city he had seen in movies, where slim, tall, angry, silent young men bashed in the heads of fat, slimy, loud-mouthed flesh-eaters like his father.

The night their mother died, coughing her guts out onto the mattress, her TB untreated, as abba cussed in orgasm inside their 'other' mother, Rahim grabbed Rahman's hand and ran.

He had watched films where boys running towards freedom from tyranny simply follow the light. The only bright lights around Akbarpur were along the railway tracks. Rahim and Rahman followed them for days and nights.

Until they reached Mumbai.

Through it all, Rahman did not utter a word. Though between the two of them, he was the one who could speak. Rahim was born dumb, his tongue stitched by God steadfast into the floor of his mouth.

Rahim never forgot how hard his heart had beaten when he had finally stopped running, staring at the thousands of people swelling this way and that, the choral murmur of their voices promising him lives he could never have had in that little junction he had come from.

Rahman's heart had broken though. The only person he cared for in the whole world was gone. He could have been tied to a post for slaughter and he wouldn't have cared.

Though in the many years that followed, the boys learnt to care for one another. It wasn't like they had a choice. They were identical. So much so that even their beards grew the same way and their hairlines receded in the exact same curves. They both belched at the same moments during their meals. And if one had a cough, rest assured the other, wherever he was, was being wracked with a phlegm attack too.

The only thing that distinguished them was a mole. On Rahman's right bum.

On some days, Rahim didn't appear when their father called out for him to come dispose of the scraps. To save them all from a thundershower of expletives, their mother would send Rahman, instructing him to not open his mouth, so their father wouldn't be able to tell it wasn't goonga Rahim. But the butcher had other ways to find that out. As Rahman would bend to pick up the chopping stump, abba would wrench his shorts off and chase the terrified boy, swinging his chopper like a woodcutter's axe, threatening to slap him on the block and slice off the mole if the boys played such tricks on him again.

Rahim would watch from the shadows, waiting for the first

dark cloud of abuses to precipitate. He would watch as Rahman would squeeze himself into a large *burni* and close the lid, making himself so small sometimes that you'd forget he even existed. And then, as abba frothed and skulked, the large invisible wind-up key jammed in his back slowly unwinding, Rahim would carelessly reveal himself, feigning ignorance of what the time was. He knew the effect he had on abba. Since he couldn't speak he was the only one abba could never squeeze a reaction out of, no matter what the intensity of his rage. And Rahim used this as a fencing sword.

He could never do that with Rahman though. Somehow, Rahman always knew what was going on inside Rahim's head. And on days when Rahim took a deep breath, silenced his furious mind and paid attention, he too could tell what was going on inside Rahman's head.

They had spent nine months joined to one another like two nostrils. That was Rahim's favourite analogy, because if one nostril got blocked, the other knew. They needed to breathe in tandem, but could breathe for each other too – which is what they grew up to do. Having worked many odd jobs across south Mumbai, and unable to save anything they earned, Rahim cracked a 'plan'. A plan which took them to the northern tip of the island city, where the land disappeared into the sea.

And took one of them with it.

2. Rahman

We aren't two, we're one, Rahman often explained to Rahim. Ammi used to say so. Rahim wasn't one for romantic notions, but even he agreed with this one, mused Rahman as he lay on the single mattress, staring at the outline maps of unknown countries being traced on the walls by white ants. He knew he should sleep, but he worried for Rahim each night. He's got abba's genes, muttered Rahman to the floor. Thank God he's goonga or he'd be cussing with every third breath. Where does all that impatience come from? Rahman had told Rahim he'd go with the pandus when they came knocking last month, but Rahim had insisted on being the martyr this time. The last time the cops had picked up Rahman and the welts they left on his legs had still not healed.

The cops had been getting increasingly frantic over the last few years. Bomb blasts had begun to hit the city with the frequency of public holidays. Before the police could wrap their heads around a bomb that blew out of a tiffin carrier near the Gateway of India, another splattered limbs from the inside of a scooter near Dadar. Casualties were far too many and suspects far too few. It seemed that Versova, the 'land's end', was inoculated from this virus. But then six months ago a taxi blew up in Vile Parle. The wheel that sprang free from the blasted cab rolled all the way past many police thanas and teetered to a halt near Versova koliwada, the fishing village, where the RDX landings were suspected to have occurred. It was only logical, the media had insisted, because after the 1980s, when Versova used to be a smuggler's favourite place to weigh anchor, it had fallen off the radar. The state's watchful eyes had since then turned to places as far off as Panvel and Mumbra, red spots on the map of the 1993 terror attack trail.

Why would these fishermen fill their fish with bomb masala, thought Rahman aloud, upset at the state's insinuations. And even if they did, what does a poor migrant autorickshaw-wallah have to do with it?

Last night, Rahman had been quiet. Rahim had poked him in the ribs to squeeze a sound out of him. The jab was futile. Rahman had finally been convinced that being picked up by the pandus five times now in less than a year was God's way of telling them that He did not approve of their deceit. On the contrary, gestured Rahim, amused, look at it this way . . . if I get locked up, you would then be free forever, because you would not officially exist. Rahim had gurgled with the exertion of his gesticulated explanation. But Rahman had felt his heart sink even further.

Rahman had never been too keen on Rahim's 'plan'. They – in fact Rahim – had applied for an autorickshaw licence. And they found themselves a little kholi out here in Khoja Gully, in the heel of the fishing village, so far from even the skeletons of the decayed boats, that on most months their landlady forgot she owned this little shack that she had to come collect the rent for. No one here knew there were two of them. They emerged one at a time. Rahim drove the rickshaw by night. And Rahman – as Rahim – drove it by day. The owner who rented his auto to Rahim had never in his thirty-year rickshaw career seen one man drive an auto both shifts, seven days a week. He was initially sceptical, worried Rahim might belly-up his three-wheeler if he falls asleep at the handle-bar. But over time, Rahim had convinced him of his 'inasmonia', explaining to him in a badly spelt, brief essay scribbled on the behind of a 'free home delivery' menu card, that he never got sleep, so he'd rather make a living on that time.

This wild lie had one downside. Rahman too had to be mute to the world outside – which meant he could only talk to Rahim, who could only talk back in gestures. Rahman was starting to forget what a real conversation felt like.

Rahim slept soundly by day. Rahman tried to sleep at night, the weight of this falsehood pressing down so hard on his heart that some invisibly connected spring kept his eyes sprung open, till the threat of dawn would inject some urgent fatigue in it and then his eyes would grudgingly close for a couple of hours each morning. This made Rahman tired. Of this life. Of being alone in what he felt. Of this strangely imposed burden of muteness. Of this unforgiving city.

And the auto.

He didn't trust the people who climbed into the passenger seat at the back every day. Most of them didn't even notice him. He could be a mere machine. They could slide money into a slot in the back of his head and he would drive them to wherever they wanted to go. The few who acknowledged him, did so only to haggle about the meter being tampered with and pay him less. To these people he was 'Rahim', hence mute. As a result of which all he could do was glower at them, hoping his stern silence would make them cough up what was his due. But silence in this city is an alien commodity. Not only is it painful in its near-total absence, but exhibiting it seems to connote to people a capitulation so complete that they step on you like you were a foot-pedal brake.

Afraid that if he ever blew a fuse a verbal projectile might launch itself out of his mouth without warning, Rahman decided to keep his passenger interactions to a bare minimum. To make that possible, he had recently bought a small slate and some chalk. Since the old meters never showed the actual fare, which had to be read off a small chart Rahim and he kept tucked above the windscreen, he had started writing the fare on the slate and holding it up for the passenger in the back. This small but determined action seemed to deter some of them from an impulsive haggle. The habitual hagglers though needed to be fed the chalk, thought Rahman, copious amounts of it! But he banished any violent thoughts as soon as they entered his head. He might be pretending to be Rahim, but he didn't want to become him. Not yet.

Also, Rahman could never figure why Rahim would need a boxful of chalk every second night when Rahman could manage a whole week on a solitary stick.

The first time he had been picked up by the pandus for interrogation was when bombs had ripped through the local trains. He remembered spending all evening ferrying the injured from Khar station to Lilavati hospital. He remembered not charging anyone a single paisa. He remembered telling the cops all of that, answering their long, violent, verbal questionnaire with countless humble nods and shakes of the head. And he remembered the sub-inspector – Doglekar was his name – saying in Marathi that all you Muslims are loose-tongued liars. And anyway, how was the police to take his word for it when he didn't even have a tongue to give his word with? Rahman was let off with a warning that time. The cops kept his licence with them, the one that referred to him as 'Rahim'. He remembered returning at 2 a.m. to see a hysterical Rahim waiting for him beside their two plates of food, both gone cold. Rahman had walked in silently, sat down, and they had eaten. One rice plate. By two. Like they always did. No fuss. No regret. No anger. Just fear. And a prayer. That tomorrow bring a little more rehmat than today.

In exchange for a week's earnings Rahim collected their licence the next evening.

Sometimes when Rahman feared for them, his nostrils would fill with the stench of dead flesh. The same smell from his father's meat shop. The smell that Rahim revelled in, but Rahman couldn't stand. It made all the fluids in his gut rise in tandem up to his throat. Every last drop. Sweet. Salty. Bitter. Cold. Hot. Sharp. Bubbling. And his head would swim. It was the stench of death. And in those precise moments what he'd regret most of all was this 'plan' of Rahim's.

To help himself through such times he'd got into the habit of keeping a small swab of cotton soaked in ittar behind his left ear. He'd scoop it out and slam it to his nose. And he'd be able to breathe again. But the ittar lingered on his whiskers till long after, and Rahim, sharp fellow that he was, would catch a whiff the minute Rahman walked in at night. And then he'd rib him about having a woman stashed away in Juhu and keeping her a secret from his dumb twin. Rahman was never amused by such talk, and earnestly defended himself, saying firstly he'd never do such things outside of marriage, and more importantly he'd never ever hide it from him. The smallest secret between the two of them could get them caught. And then he'd proceed to tell Rahim every last detail of the day. It was a habit they'd cultivated ever since they'd got that rickshaw licence. Since they were to be one person by day and night, they needed to know all there was to know about each other, so that they never got caught off guard.

But there was one small embarrassing detail Rahman never shared with Rahim. On those days when even the ittar was of no use and he felt himself shivering in a fever of fear, Rahman would end his day early, park the auto behind the abandoned boats outside Khoja Gully, lift the back seat, empty the little chamber there of their tools of repair, climb in, and slide the seat back into place above him. Scrunched up in a foetal position in there, he would then think of ammi, and the nine months he had spent inside of her, and of which he had no memory. For those few dark, breathless, unending minutes that womb would be his alone, not shared with one exactly like him. His ammi would then be alive, and he'd be unborn, waiting to live. Sometimes he'd lie there till he gagged. Sometimes he'd lie there till his legs cramped. Most times he'd just lie there till he could weep no more. And then he'd climb out, his fear washed off, his mother's death accepted. He would replace the tools, the seat and drive back home.

As Rahman lay watching the first few fingers of dawn slowly taking hold of his eyelids and pulling them down over his watchful eyes, he had a sinking feeling. *I hope the cops don't take Rahim this time*, he muttered into his shapeless pillow. *Ever since they interrogated him the last time, he's been so short-tempered and distant. If they come knocking, I'll find a way to reason with them. And we'll leave this place, this gully of the lost. This city of the unfortunate. We'll run again. I'll lead this time. And where we go, we can live fearlessly as two. Not one, by two, like we do here.*

And just as his eyes slid shut, a key rattled nervously in the lock on the door outside. Rahim, shaking, tumbled in, and with his hands doing a manic dance in mid-air he signed out, 'Bhai, there's been a blast in Borivli.'

3. Ramdulari

The first time Rahim had gone missing from the streets he'd taken his hands off the handlebar in response to Ramdulari's query, and joined his fingertips to gesture 'home'. And where's that, she had asked, snapping her powder-case shut, not convinced. Far away, Rahim had indicated dramatically, a small railway junction where no one ever stops, he had gesticulated slowly in the rear-view mirror. The complete opposite of Mumbai, she had added, everyone's last stop. Rahim had smiled triumphantly. He had taught her the sign language over the many months he had known her. And she had learnt well.

The second time he had gone missing, he signalled to her that he had been sick. What with, she had asked concerned. He paused. It was a cold night. He fogged up the mirror with his breath, and with his finger, scrawled 'loveria', chuckling. Ramdulari had taken over a dozen customers that night to spite his blatant lie, and watched his drawn face in the smudgy mirror with one eye as she got fingered and squeezed.

Both times Langdi had been off the roads for a few nights.

Rahim never missed work if he could help it. In the hallowed circles of the rickshaw-wallahs he was nicknamed '*duronto*', after the new non-stop long-distance train to Calcutta that hurtled through day and night without any stops to reach its passengers to their destination. Now, *this* Rahman didn't mind. All said and done, it did feel powerful to be the possessors of a secret that no one else in the whole world would ever be privy to.

Or so he thought.

The last time Langdi disappeared, Ramdulari had heard that Rahim had been picked up for pooch-taach in connection with the bomb blasts that very day. Fist-fucking the right pandu revealed to her that Rahim had been a regular suspect, picked up by the cops every time there was a round of interrogations. She went cold down to her tailbone. The five times she had been compelled to hire another auto as her mobile 'full-tension-release' shag-pad had coincided with the bomb blasts in the city. Not only were customers hard to come by on those nights, she even had to pay by the meter, something Rahim never made her do. She had a lot to be pissed with Rahim for.

When Rahim returned last month, he sidled Langdi up to Ramdulari at the corner of Panch Marg and tried to apologize for disappearing. 'My house got washed away in the high tide,' read his slate as he held it up in front of her face, his smile a precarious mix of cocky and earnest. She had merely looked past him at the mobile police-patrol motorbike cruising by across the road, turned and hurried away. She didn't want to be seen with him. The hafta she already owed the cops far exceeded what she'd made in the last week. If she got caught in a terror suspect's auto they might harass her for some more. And she'd heard of how they tortured female 'suspects'. The pandu had told her, as she gave him a handjob inside a broken down car behind the chowki, getting off on the memory of the last time he fucked an upside down woman with his laathi. Though he did add he'd hate to do something like that to Ramdulari, there was no remorse or mercy in his voice when he spoke of the 'suspect', emphatically adding that the 'minority' needed to be hung upside down and straightened out. At that he had ejaculated, spitting venom all over the dusty dashboard.

Rahim followed Ramdulari down the street, braking to a halt every few seconds to clean his slate and scribble a new request on it with chalk, before revving up again, gliding alongside her and holding the slate up in front of her face, begging her to get inside, saying he'd drive her around for free tonight. She ignored him completely, a knot forming in her chest, her face flushed. But

Rahim kept at it. He kept at it till he ran out of chalk. And then he hit the brakes, wiped his slate clean, and sat still, watching her disappear down the street, his hands starting to ache as the flat rectangular piece of night they held grew heavy with the weight of its own wordlessness.

After that night, every night, for nearly a month, Ramdulari kept her distance. Rahim would catch glimpses of her in other rickshaws, as he ferried drunk young boys, watchful dupatta-covered women and zombie-like call-centre employees back and forth. When his shift ended, tired and irritable, he'd make do with the fast-fading memory of that meagre morning. The one in which Ramdulari had stepped out of the circular margin of the rear-view mirror and invited him into the back seat.

It had been the night after his first reappearance, and customers – scared by the terror unleashed on Mumbai's streets – were nowhere to be found. Strapped for cash and feeling unwanted, Ramdulari had suggested she pay Rahim in kind. Rahim had never dared to insinuate that to her. He was both thrilled and terrified at the invitation. He hadn't touched a woman before, and he shyly indicated that to her. She had simply nodded. He had parked Langdi right in the centre of an abandoned field amidst a far off cluster of cottages in Aaraamnagar. The risqué move had made Ramdulari hot. As the moon slipped out of the sky, he had slipped into her. But he had finished even before the cock had crowed. She had sighed 'premachoor', and patted him on the head. He didn't know what it meant, but knew it didn't bode well for his future with her.

And he was right.

He often hoped she'd make that offer again, give him another chance to prove he could gratify her. But she never did, pretending instead as if that morning had never existed. She had however started talking more, telling Rahim about her life, and why she thought 'tension-releasers' like herself were so important in Mumbai's scheme of things. He didn't care much to listen, but listened well, in the hope that one night she might feel some love and send it his way.

'If it wasn't for us,' she used to say, 'there'd be many more old women with knives in their bellies and young girls lying raped in alleys. We Ramdularis help release the beasts you men keep locked up inside you.' With that she'd light her only cigarette of the night, lean out of the auto, and leave a trail of smoke like a sad, small cirrus cloud.

Over the course of the month Rahim started to simmer. It wasn't a feeling he was familiar with, but he couldn't help it. Rahman noticed it. But the few times he attempted to talk about it with Rahim, an invisible door was slammed shut in his face. Rahman felt scared for Rahim. They had never been this far apart before. 'The next time the cops come for us, if, God-forbid, they do,' he had told Rahim, 'promise me, you'll allow *me* to go.' Surprisingly for Rahman, Rahim readily nodded. He even looked relieved. Rahim had not forgotten how he had smarted when that sub-inspector Doglekar had abused his community. But Rahman wanted to forgive and move on. Rahim however possessed no such reservoir inside himself that he could dip into. He signed a 'thank you' to his brother and got up quickly so that Rahman wouldn't see the film that had spread over his eyes.

The brothers decided to carry on with their normal life despite the Borivli blast. Disappearing now would make the cops unnecessarily suspicious. Not like they needed a reason to.

Rahman stopped by the Yari Road masjid thrice to pray that day. He felt confident God was having a change of heart.

But the next morning, Rahim didn't return.

Rahman, though restless, his heart beating like the drums of Muharram, stayed put at home. The smell of death returned stronger than ever to his nostrils. He tried to shrug it off, talking to himself, telling himself that the stench must be from all the dead fish being dried in the fishing gaon. But his voice couldn't convince his ears.

On the second day, there was a sharp rap on the door. Rahman's breath froze. He didn't respond. The knocking continued. A voice, scathing with authority, called out, 'Rahim?' Rahman clenched his eyes shut. A part of him wanted to know where Rahim was. And perhaps this voice could tell him. But the other part of him told him to not expose himself. What if this was a trick, aimed at blowing their cover? 'Damn the plan, damn me, why did I ever listen to Rahim,' Rahman muttered into his cold, sweating fist.

On the third flurry of knocks, Rahman, shaking, opened the window. Doglekar stood outside. Rahman's throat went dry when the cop, his eyes hidden behind cheap plastic shades, pointed at the lock on the door outside and asked, 'Trying to avoid the landlord?' Rahman mustered a weak smile and nodded. Doglekar handed him their licence and said, 'You left it at the thana that night.' As Rahman gently took it from him, Doglekar seemed to peer at him as if searching for a piece that didn't fit.

And then he turned and left.

That night Rahman emerged, feverish and fearful, gagging on the imagined smell of rotting flesh. His cache of ittar had vapourized a while back. He now needed some sea air to wash the stink away. Worse, all the Bisleri bottles inside the room had already filled with his piss, and now he needed to shit and get something to eat. To get his mind off Rahim, he tried to remember the taste of dal chaawal. All he'd eaten in two days was stale pav and dried chillis. He took the path that led to the beach; he wanted to be seen by as few people as possible.

Returning with a rice plate packed in flimsy plastic, the thought of not needing to 'by two' it was starting to depress him when he saw her . . . at the mouth of Khoja Gully: Langdi, leaning slightly on the raised footpath, as if waiting for him.

4. Langdi

Rahman inhabited Langdi on the third day. He had tried not to, but he had run out of money, and the rickshaw owner had sent him a warning to drive or go fuck his mother. Missing Rahim desperately, he gave in, and for the first time ever, he spoke to the auto, calling her 'Langdi' just as Rahim used to, hoping that being friendly with the lame one might make her spit out a clue to his brother's whereabouts. When Rahman lovingly wrenched her starting lever, black and yellow Langdi spat out nothing except for a thick vomit of smoke from her rear: she was overdue on her PUC.

The smell of decaying flesh now burned through his entire being. That evening, on his way back after a fruitless day spent waiting for passengers in the October heat, he had screeched to a halt before the large tree in the centre of the road and puked all over its roots. He desperately wanted to crawl into the auto's belly beneath the back seat but Langdi seemed oddly unwelcoming. In the face of her uninviting stoicism then, Rahman said to himself,

'I have to be brave. I can't get weak now. What if Rahim needs me?' And with that thought, he denied himself the cosiness of his ammi's imagined womb.

He bought himself full rice plates every night, and saved exactly half of everything, packing it back into the little plastic bags the sabzi, dal, rotis, rice, onion and pickle had come in. 'You never know when Rahim walks in through that door,' he'd say to himself, 'what if he's hungry?' With the passing days, the packets of stale food began to accumulate, stacked up in a messy corner of the single-room kholi like a miniature memorial to the missing twin. In time, the room too began to smell like something had died inside it.

A passenger commented on the stench one evening. 'Did someone die in here?' he asked as he squirmed in the back seat. Rahman, stunned, asked aloud, 'You can smell it?' The old man nodded, staring at Rahman as if he'd seen a ghost, then asked, 'You can speak?' And Rahman realized what he had done. This was a man who hailed his auto every Saturday – his off-day – to take him to Juhu beach, to let the sea wash away his desiccated solitude. And now, in one brief moment of confusion, Rahman had destroyed what Rahim and he had taken nearly four years to construct.

They continued their journey in a strange cloud of silence. When the man got off, he paid Rahman, and waddled away, vigorously dusting his hands, cleaning them of the dirt of deceit he had been party to for so long. Rahman was done with the day.

The next time Rahman took Langdi out was at night. And as soon as he turned the corner near the Hanuman Mandir, he was flagged down by Ramdulari. He tried to drive past. Rahman was choosy about whom he allowed into his vehicle. He was not going to let a sex worker sit atop his mother's womb. But Ramdulari seemed desperate. She didn't just stick her hand out like others do, she stood square in his path. Before Rahman could change his mind, she scurried into the auto. Rahman sat still for several long moments wondering if he should ask the sex worker to get off. Ramdulari too sat still for several long moments, feeling guilty, unable to phrase the beginnings of a conversation inside her head. Just as Rahman turned to her, his cheeks smarting, she sputtered, 'I'm sorry.' Rahman's eyes went round. There was a dark tinge of familiarity in her tone. Rahim! She must know him. She might even know where he might be. So Rahman veiled his ignorance and enthusiasm and gestured, 'What for?'

'I know you must be mad at me,' Ramdulari said, 'I was scared … scared the cops might implicate me too if they saw me with someone they suspected of being a terrorist.'

When he heard that, Rahman couldn't veil his sadness. 'I'm so relieved to see you,' she continued, looking genuinely pleased, 'I thought they might have … you know … "encounter"ed you or something.' And her gaze dropped to the floor. A long moment slowly passed between them, thick and heavy with their private despairs, and then Rahman gestured, 'Where can I take you?' smiling gently. It was unlike any smile she had ever got out of Rahim. She said 'Aaraamnagar' and smiled back mischievously. Rahman, confused, turned back to the handlebar, twisted the accelerator, and made his mind speed through all the possible ways he could broach the subject of Rahim without arousing the lady's suspicions.

She made him stop in the centre of the field, reached over and killed the engine, her breasts spilling onto Rahman's frail shoulder. Rahman protested. But she shut his mouth with a kiss, unlocking their lips as soon as she had locked them, shying away and waiting for her 'Rahim' to take it from there. What she heard instead was a loud, alarmed 'Lahaulwillaquwat!' and looked up to see a red-faced Rahman, his eyes bursting with furious tears, his lips trembling, glaring at her with an agitated mixture of distress and shock. 'You … you can speak?' she asked, on the brink of tears.

It was the second time in as many days that Rahman had been slapped with that question. But he didn't realize that then. Instead he stuttered and gesticulated in a confused attempt at coherence, 'Rahim and y-you … you a-and Rahim?' Before Ramdulari could figure how to react, he said, 'Please … request … get off … PLEASE!'

And she did. Standing alone, cold and bewildered, she watched the man she thought was mute – was Rahim – rev the auto up like a raging beast and lurch into the darkness. She didn't know what just happened. Her heart squeezed so tight that she didn't know if she ever wanted to know either.

'How could he not tell me?' shrieked Rahman silently, 'how could I not have figured it out?' He used to be able to read Rahim's mind. Rahim had admitted it. *That's why perhaps. The sly chutiya, had made that admission to make me overconfident, so that I'd think that I can read his mind, when in reality he hid things in its little corners that I'd never be able to reach, unless he allowed me to.* And now he finds out that Rahim never did allow him.

For nearly an hour, Rahman drove around like a crazed bull, missing ramming into cars and buses by mere millimetres. When he was spent, the fuel gauge nudging 'E', he killed the engine, glided down the sandy incline to the far end of Khoja Gully, braked dead behind the dead boat, muttered 'I can't take it any more' and looked at the back seat, urging himself to step inside his ammi. And as he lifted the back seat, he saw inside – scrunched up in a foetal position – Rahim, decayed almost to the bone.

5. Khoja

Abba chopped a big chunk of meat into little boti-boti. Beside him lay the other pieces of Rahim's body, segregated neatly, like a goat's at Eid. He scraped the little chopped bits off the stump into a bag and looked up at little Rahim. Ammi sat on the ground nearby and wailed loudly, mourning the death of her voiceless son.

Little Rahim stood on the dirty hill overlooking the railway tracks. He had the bag full of little bits of his own adult meat before him. He tossed the pieces up into the air absently, as large eagles, the expanse of their wings blotting out the sun, swooped down and grabbed the pieces as they soared up towards them.

The stench was unbearable.

But Rahman, curled up on Langdi's back seat, was getting used to it. He inhaled long and deep, thinking how he could never do what abba, ammi or Rahim would have – chop, mourn or dispose of. Honestly, he didn't even care any more how Rahim must have died. In fact, all he felt now was rage. A suppressed, implosive rage. At the betrayal. Not only had Rahim hidden the most important part of his life from him, he had now snatched away his last refuge, their mother's womb, the only thing – the only thing in the whole world Rahman had coveted as his own. Not to be by/two-ed.

But it had now been done.

Rahman pushed the auto, its fuel tank run dry, to the same turning where he had found it last week. He stepped back and looked at it one last time, leaning on the pavement, waiting to be found again. And when he looked above it he saw a sign that read 'Khoja', as if instructing him to 'be lost'.

Lost.

Who was he any more? He wondered aloud.

Rahim?

Rahman?

Neither of the two?

Rahim alone had been proof that Rahman was real. With him gone, who remained? The Rahim Rahman pretended to be? Or Rahman, who no one knew – or would believe – ever existed.

Rahman wondered. Louder and louder. Not caring if anyone heard. He was done with being mute. He spoke all the way back to his little hellhole. Once inside, he continued speaking. For all the years he hadn't spoken. About all the things he always wanted to say, but never could. He spoke. And he spoke. And he spoke. Through fits of hacking cough. Through day and night. Through hunger and a raging fever. He spoke.

Until there was a sharp knocking on his door once again.

6. Doglekar

The Borivli blast had left Rahim terrified. At the crossing of Seven Bungalows, the images of blown-up bodies tumbling through his mind, he had jumped a signal. So distracted was he that he didn't even notice when a pandu on a bike started to trail him. It was only when the bike angled its nose sharply across his path did he hit the brakes and feel his heart freeze with fear.

In seconds his licence was gone. In minutes he found himself before Doglekar once more. The name on the challan had popped up in the system as a suspect in the blasts. And the RTO had spun him around and sent him to the same chowki he or Rahman had visited five times that year.

Standing before the raisin-faced SI once more, Rahim didn't know why but he thought of Ramdulari, and how this time when he returned to the streets with Langdi, she would never turn to look at him ever again. His mind wandering, once again he lost track of where he was. By now he had missed answering two questions shot at him by the SI. And even as he collected his wits, a heavy slap slammed into the side of his face. Bouncing back off the floor, burning with indignation, Rahim didn't know why, but he slapped Doglekar right back!

The next thing he knew he was being beaten by a rifle butt, a different bone cracking under the weight of each blow. Growing dizzy with what must have been the loss of blood, he did what any normal person would do – any normal person who had broken the law: he confessed.

At first, he gesticulated feverishly, trying to tell Doglekar that there were – not one – but two of them, but Doglekar understood nothing. Desperate, Rahim – his mind a blur of red rage and yellow fear – lunged for a notepad and pen on Doglekar's desk. At which point the SI slammed the blunt edge of the rifle into Rahim's ribs. Rahim hung by the precipice of the desk, numb to the hammering, choosing his words painfully, pinning them down one by one on the paper sheet, trying to tell Doglekar in the only way he could that he ... and his identical twin ... drove one autorickshaw ... by day and by night ... only for some extra income ... and that they were not terrorists ... and that he was sorry … very, very sorry … for breaking the law … they would pay for it … swear on God … but to please stop beating him now … or he might die. At that, Rahim had slipped off the edge and crumpled to the floor, the pen's nib puncturing the page.

The last thing Rahim remembered was Doglekar kicking him in the mouth as he lay smashed and bleeding on the floor. Doglekar had simply said 'katua'.

And then Rahim's broken heart had stopped ticking.

For a good minute, heaving from the exertion of his workout, Doglekar hadn't realized what had just happened. Then he bent over and checked Rahim's breathing. There was none. 'Bhenchod!' he had muttered, his blood going cold. And then he had lunged for the sheet of 'rubbish' the 'pimp' had scribbled on, and as he frantically made sense of it, his back slowly straightened and a sigh of relief escaped from between his raspy breath.

7. By/Two

Rahman answered the door. Two policemen stood outside, grimacing at the stench.

'Rahim?' they asked.

Rahman nodded.

'Is that your auto?' they asked, pointing at Langdi, half-hanging from the hook of a tow truck, fresh for display in abba's meat shop.

Rahman nodded.

'We found a dead body inside,' the cop said.

To which Rahman nodded again and muttered, 'That was Rahman,' and held his hands out to be led away.

1 BHK

He wouldn't rent the flat out to a Muslim, he said, and asked me for some proof of my identity.

There was a hairline crack in the kitchen wall. It looked like a geographical boundary line from some map.

One of the walls sang a throbbing Marathi folk song. Every window let in a different smell.

'If the doors aren't latched,' he said, 'they slam in the breeze.'

The drain was laced with a cobweb similar to the steel grill covering it.

The entrance faced the west.

RED, 17

Working at a laundry had its perks. Sifting, folding, unfolding, packing clothes could be strangely therapeutic. Ever since his wife died in the bomb blast three years ago, Nandu had been working at Rangat Laundry. The blast had spared his life, but not his hearing. This job was the only one that would have him after he lost his constable's uniform. What use would he be as a protector of the public if he couldn't *hear* the voice of the junta? But the police force was kind to him; he still got a monthly pension. And he was free to spend all day at Rangat, quietly tending to other people's second skins, skins that came in worse for wear and emerged good as new.

On most days, they emerged under his arm.

He spent the evenings delivering the laundered clothes to their respective owners. It was a responsibility he enjoyed, ensuring that his customers would turn out crisp, clean and creaseless the next morning. But it wasn't a duty he romanticized the way his boss Liyaqat did.

To Liyaqat – the ageing owner of Rangat – laundering was a way of permanently cleansing the clothing of the leftover auras of the past, so that it would glow with the wearer's aura anew. He had inherited the philosophy from his father who had established Rangat in 1938.

Nandu liked the foolish self-importance of the old world. The new world attached value to nothing. He had spent over a thousand afternoons behind the Burma teak-wood counter in the shop trying to acquaint himself with the people from the clothes they left behind ... thinking of his dead wife Hamida ... the fateful local train ride ... his thirteen-year-old son Baiju ... and the promise he had made his wife: getting Baiju a special gift for Eid this year.

When Baiju was born, Nandu and Hamida had decided that they would celebrate Diwali and Eid with equal pomp each year so that their child could have the best of both. But in the last two years after Hamida's death, Nandu guiltily admitted he had cheated ... he ended up spending all his savings on Diwali and by the time Eid came around there was no money left to buy Baiju anything.

The day after tomorrow is Eid. Which makes the appearance of this coat as rare as an Eid ka chaand, thought Nandu to himself. There was a number stitched into the inside of the collar. '17'. That would make the old man, Feroze, one of Rangat's oldest customers.

Nandu let his rough fingers glide gently over the wool. It was an old coat, no doubt. There wasn't a single ready-made shop in the city that sold such a delightful knit any more. If they did, the coats were branded. And this one wasn't. The only identity this coat carried was the '17' cross-stitched intricately with a deep red thread inside the elegant collar. Nandu closed his eyes as his fingers trailed the little loops in the 17. Back in the 1970s, when this coat must have come in to Rangat for a laundering, Liyaqat bhai must have sat down behind this same counter when the shop shut, and stitched the customer number in. I would have made a 17 in barely ten pokes of the needle, thought Nandu. Jaisa daam, vaisa kaam. But Liyaqat bhai must have taken over ten minutes. And then he would have tugged at each little loop with his needle to check if it was a steadfast stitch. Liyaqat bhai. Tch. For him, life lasts forever. So everything he touches should last forever too.

Nandu stepped back, looked at the coat one last time, then started folding it. A cool wind caught the back of his neck from the door and he looked around guiltily to check if no one had seen him lusting after the coat like that. Folded, the dark coat looked handsome. From an angle to the left, the coat was jet black. But when seen from a similar angle to the right, it magically turned into a deep ink blue. Nandu looked wistful. He had tried not to think the thought several times in the last few minutes, but it burst like a balloon filled past its capacity, into his mind now. Feroze was a slight man.

His coat would fit Baiju perfectly.

The crinkly brown-paper parcel changed shapes under his arm as Nandu walked. Thanks to the Maharashtra Police, Baiju's playing basketball in his break time in a convent school, thought Nandu. Or else he'd be squandering his hours over a carrom board outside a municipal school. Baiju will be the commissioner of police some day. Nandu startled the lady beside him by saying that out loud. He smiled at her helplessly. He could never tell when a thought escaped from his lips without warning. It was a joke his dead ears played on him often. The happy thought made Nandu's feet move faster and he almost broke into a trot.

The Friday namaaz had just got over in the nearby mosque. Wading through the colourful crowd, he stopped at a chaiwallah to ask for directions to the address on the little chit. He held his spectacles in the steam from the boiling tea for a moment and then wiped the lens with his shirt. He blinked hard as he placed them back on his nose. He had learned to rely on his eyes more and more in the last three years. He had learnt to 'hear' with them.

He remembered Liyaqat noting that all the 'red' customers had learnt to rely on washing machines years ago. Feroze, though, had taken his laundering to some other laundry. The sight of that red 17 had made Liyaqat wistful. He had told Nandu that in 1978 when the customer base touched 1,000, he had switched to a blue thread. Feroze's coat was the first 'red' he'd seen in a decade. It seemed like he had never subjected that beautiful coat to a 'top-loaded tumble-dry'. And thank God for that, said Liyaqat, oddly ecstatic. He was eager to return to the coat its original rangat. Nandu shook his head indulgently at the memory of that conversation and, though he tried not to, he thought of Baiju again.

And then he turned a corner and froze.

There before him was the building Al Husseini mentioned on the chit. It seemed nearly as old as Rangat. In every window and doorway were clusters of women and children, looking solemn. Nandu squeezed his way past a small crowd stuck like flies to the gate and saw a corpse, covered in rose petals, on a stretcher about to be hoisted into a corpse van. Nandu seemed to be the only spot of colour floating in the sea of black. He stepped up to the only man there who didn't look grief-struck and inquired, 'Bhai, Feroze Aslam?' The man looked at him gravely and nodded. Nandu looked at him for a long awkward moment, and then it hit him . . . the janaaza was Feroze's! The man looked vacantly up at the first floor and said, 'He was a good man, a very good man.'

Nandu looked at Feroze's dead face ... then at the brown parcel in his hand ... and then he thought of Baiju. Closing his eyes for a long moment he tried to shut out any thoughts of his son. And when he opened his eyes, Feroze had been slid into the van. The funeral procession was leaving the courtyard slowly. Nandu didn't know why but he found himself checking the height and build of each of the men in that courtyard as they filed out solemnly behind the van. They were all either heavy-set, broad-shouldered or tall, or all of the above. One of the last to exit was a frail middle-aged man, slim, stooped, his eyes unblinking, his hair a shock of white. He seemed like he'd fit into the coat, thought Nandu, as he walked alongside him. 'Were you related to Feroze?' asked Nandu genuinely. 'No,' replied the man, pondering each word like he would a morsel, 'I repair his watches.' Nandu read his lips.

'That's sad,' said Nandu. The man looked, alarmed. Nandu pointed at the funeral procession, 'That he's passed, its sad.'

'I think so,' said the man strangely, and turned and walked away from Nandu and the funeral. Again, Nandu thought of Baiju, stopped by the side, closed his eyes, folded his hands, said a small prayer, wedged the parcel under his arm, turned and left.

'Take the wheat to the chakki, Baiju,' said Nandu, chopping onions and crying copious tears. Slender Baiju turned the TV off immediately, entered the kitchen blinking hard and picked up the thaili of wheat . . . and stopped. 'Why're you crying, baba?'

he asked, exaggerating his words, so his father would read them. Nandu smiled and pointed at the onions. 'But they never made you cry before,' said Baiju.

'They allow you a winter blazer from class nine, no?' asked Nandu. 'Uh – yes, but I'll wear the sweater only, don't worry, I don't feel that cold,' said Baiju hoisting the thaili over his shoulder and slipping his feet into his chappals.

'This year you will,' said Baiju, soaking his tears into the shoulder of his shirt.

Baiju looked at him strangely. 'It never even gets cold in Mumbai, baba,' he said, and left.

Nandu unpacked the coat from the brown paper, unfolded it and hung it on the only wooden hanger in the old steel almirah where he had still stored all his wife's salwaar-kameezes and jewellery. He folded the wrapping, rolled up the thread that had been used to tie the package, and neatly kept them both on the shelf below. Nandu wasted nothing. He believed everything outlasts us. It's us, just us, that don't last forever. The paper would come in handy. So would the thread. For what exactly, I'm not sure, thought Nandu, but come in handy it will. In just the same way the coat is going to serve Baiju now that Feroze Aslam has passed. Is that wrong? I don't know. Can a coat 'belong' to a dead man?

That last thought brought Nandu some strength. He liked logic. It filled up the void that emotional turmoil always left behind. It was logic that helped him cope with his wife's death. It was logic that gave him the strength to deal with a world where there was no music. As long as he was alive, he'd have to eat three times a day, sleep six hours every night, bathe, brush his teeth and tend to his son. It was all logical. It had to be done.

Heartache and sadness drained him. But logic filled him with hope. And it was logic that said to him in a firm set of words that he could hear – 'A. Dead. Man. Does. Not. Need. A. Coat.'

But why then – thought Nandu, as he ate quietly – do I still feel this emptiness? Baiju's eyes were glued to the small colour TV. On the screen Dhoni was on strike. On top of the TV were Nandu, Hamida and six-year-old Baiju sitting on a horse at Juhu Chowpatty.

'Too much salt,' muttered Nandu at the food, and got up.

The next day was the longest day he'd ever spent inside the cosy confines of Rangat. He sifted the clothes that had come in without lingering over them for too long, he folded the laundered clothes in a hurry, packed them even faster. He didn't want to hear any of the stories that the clothes carried today. He didn't want to guess the kind of people that wore them. He wanted to be distant from them all, from their joys and their losses, their lives and deaths. He tried, for the first time in three years, to *just* do his job. Liyaqat didn't notice. Liyaqat noticed nothing in the world that was outside of the clothes he tended to. Nandu thought Liyaqat might not even miss him if he were to not come in to work some day. He'd just wait and then hire someone else.

Liyaqat was certainly not going to miss a dead man's coat.

That evening Nandu walked so fast that he finished all five deliveries in under an hour. He stopped for a glass of cutting chai. And with the first sip of the ginger-drenched milky tea, his mind slowed down. First thing tomorrow, I'll give the coat to Baiju – his Eid gift, he told himself, and the smile on his face when he wears it to school, shows it off to his friends . . . that smile will warm Feroze's heart wherever he may be now.

But that thought brought with it another question: 'Do the dead feel? And if they do, might Feroze miss that coat?'

No. The dead don't feel. The dead don't drink tea. The dead certainly don't miss their coats. Because the dead don't feel the winter chill.

Or the lack of it in Mumbai.

Baiju was still fast asleep when Nandu crept out of bed. Nandu hadn't been able to sleep all night with the excitement of the gift. He walked extra slowly, watching the floor, worried that if he knocked something he wouldn't hear it but Baiju would, and he didn't want Baiju to wake up till much later.

Nandu took the coat off the hanger, and lovingly ran his wiry, weather-beaten fingers all over the coat's breast again. He'd lost count of how many times he'd done that since the previous evening. Then he carried it stylishly to the room where his wife's picture hung on the wall. He held the coat up for her to inspect, and hoped she'd be able to smell it despite the sandalwood garland that surrounded her photo frame. He said to her, 'From this Eid, our son's going to look like a commissioner.' He was careful not to move his lips too much lest he speak too loud. And anyway, I'm sure Hamida can hear my thoughts, he thought to himself.

And then he froze.

The dead don't need coats.

The dead can't hear thoughts.

And a strange emptiness returned, pushed a tear out of his eye.

He felt a little dizzy. He didn't like this: it didn't seem 'logical'. What was he doing with a dead man's coat that didn't belong to him? What was he doing talking to his dead wife? But then, he thought, just because she's dead doesn't mean she can't feel what I feel. I speak to her every day and it warms my heart. Why is this any different? Can she hear me?

Can a dead man miss his favourite coat?

Nandu walked the fastest he had ever walked in his whole life. In a few minutes he was running. The brown-paper package beneath his arm changed form viciously with the exertion of his run. The paper tore in a couple of places exposing the wool of the coat inside. And as the 5 a.m. azaan slowly drifted up with the dawn sun, the coat shimmered a mysterious dark blue. Nandu ran through the gates of Al Husseini and quickly grunted up the creaking wooden stairs.

Noor sat in a throne-like cane chair at the large table. The coat lay unfolded on the table before her. She looked at it like a first-time mother would at her just-delivered baby.

Noor was plump. The kind of soft, glowing, taut plump that age cannot ripen with wrinkles. But she was old. The laugh lines on either side of her eyes had evidently gone out of use only recently. She touched the coat lightly, as if expecting it to vanish under her fingers. When it didn't, she pressed her chubby, soft fingers down on it and let them run along the weave. Nandu sat in a chair across from her. He was quiet. A cup before him held tea that had formed a thick brown film on its surface.

And then as he watched, Noor started folding the coat up, said 'thank you', placed it in the brown paper, folded that over the coat neatly, tied it with the thread, forming an elegant shoelace knot and pushed the parcel towards Nandu.

'I . . .' stuttered Nandu.

Noor smiled sadly. 'Feroze had given his favourite camel-skin shoes to his old cobbler the previous day. And his gold HMT watch to the only man who refuses to repair a watch unless he gets the original spare parts.'

'I – I don't understand,' stuttered Nandu. That appeared to remind Noor of something and she apologized and was about to start saying that again with gesticulations this time, when Nandu said, 'No, no, I followed what you said, but I didn't understand. I – I *stole* his coat . . .'

'No,' said Noor, 'he *wanted* you to have it. He was a pragmatic man. He believed that our things outlive us. So he left his prized possessions in those places where he knew they'd be looked after. He knew he was going to leave for his final holy journey on the last day of this Ramzan.'

'How do you know?' asked Nandu slightly bewildered.

'He still speaks to me,' said Noor and smiled again. 'Would you like me to heat the tea up for you?' Nandu just shook his head dumbly, gulped the tea down, picked up the package, said a hurried 'thank you' and ran out of the door.

Baiju stood before the large mirror on the wall in Rangat, beaming. Liyaqat watched very curiously as the tailor from the neighbouring shop stretched the measuring tape from Baiju's left shoulder to his right, then turned to the coat – kept open on the counter – and made some marks on it with blue chalk. A beaming Nandu held Baiju by his chin, smiled and said, 'Eid mubaarak, bachcha.' But Baiju simply asked, 'You brought it that day when you were crying, no?'

'What?' said Nandu, taken by surprise.

'I saw you put it in ammi's cupboard, but I didn't want to ruin your surprise,' said Baiju shyly. Nandu's eyes moistened over as he grabbed his boy and hugged him tight. 'And it wasn't the onions, no?' asked Baiju, laughing.

'You know everything,' said Nandu and playfully pushed him out of the shop. Behind them the tailor settled onto a stool next to two glasses of chai.

'Nandu,' called out Liyaqat, his brow collecting knits by the second. Baiju stopped Nandu in his tracks, gestured to him that he was being called inside. Nandu poked his head in through the door. Liyaqat took a moment to frame his thoughts, peered at Nandu inquisitively and said, 'This is the red 17.' As if that statement was question enough, he said nothing after it, choosing, instead, to wait for a reply.

'Yes,' said Nandu, 'an Eid ka chaand. Should we change it to blue, now?'

OCCUPYING SILENCE

He had the window seat. I sat at the other end of the same berth.

The small fan *gadh-gadh-gadh-gadh*-ed overhead very slowly. Everyone else had been rocked to sleep.

I liked being scared by the sudden boom of a diesel engine hurtling past.

When he got up to go to the toilet, I crawled over to the window on all fours and let the hot wind attack my face. Every other sound suddenly died.

SEVEN SUNDAYS

One

At daybreak, I am three.

Half asleep, I smell the Margo soap, hear dull thumps as she waddles from the bath to her bed near the window, and see her glistening wet, silver-thready hair through slightly open eyes. A mattress placed across three identical iron trunks makes up her bed. I hear the trunk hinges groan under her weight as she thumps herself down.

As she pulls the curtains apart, I turn over in my bed and pull my sheet over my head. She slips her dentures into her mouth. As they slip snug onto her gums, the wrinkles above her lip grow taut. She nestles her back into the fold in the wall, props up her behind with her pillow, leans her head to one side and settles down to watch them from her window.

Half the view from the first-floor window is shrouded by a mango tree. In the other half are distant drenched men of all sizes, shapes and ages, Hooghly river water gushing out of a hole in the ground, and lots of soap lather.

She watches Raja sitting on the pavement with his legs spread wide, trying to coerce some lather out of soap and a bald head. She watches Kaalia's long bony arms soap points on his back that no normal arm can ever reach. And then she watches Rafiq rub soap vigorously all over his four-year-old son's trembling body. She watches Hussein dunk a tin can into the water and splash himself over and over again. She giggles to herself when Pappu's slippery soap leaps out of his hurried hands and disappears into the drain. And she looks away abashedly when Jimmy's hand scrubs around under his wet lungi.

Suddenly the gush stops.

A few pairs of soap-covered eyes blink open helplessly. Kaalia checks his waterproof watch and curses. Three heads turn to Hussein's full can and then look longingly as Hussein empties it very slowly over his head.

She yawns, draws the curtains closed, shifts the pillow from under her bottom, unfolds onto her back, and covers her head with the pallu of her white saree, humming a shabad hymn to herself.

'Daadi?' I groan, 'let me slee-eep.'

And the song stops.

Two

In the morning, I am four.

When we walk through New Market, I look down at the tops of people's heads. I have a bird's-eye view of Lal uncle's bald patch. He'll never be able to lie to us about it ever again. I touch the signboards of shops without having to even stretch my arm. I casually look into a basket of fruits on a porter's head. I almost steal an orange, but he looks up into my eyes and hurries away.

We stop for a minute as I play the tabla on the roof of an Ambassador car. On Chowringhee, I can see as far as Dharmatala over everyone's heads. Only a double-decker bus manages to block my view. When the bus stops, I look in through the window to see if there are any empty seats. Normally it's hard to do that unless you're six-and-a-half-feet tall.

But I am no normal kid.

I have Suresh chacha. Six feet two, with shoulders so wide that it feels like a bench when he makes me sit on them. Our combined height is nearly seven feet.

When we climb into the bus my head knocks against the conductor's bell in the roof, and the bus starts with a sudden lurch.

Three

At noon, I am nine.

I am startled awake by a vigorously beating drum. The page I have fallen asleep over has been crushed under the weight of my head, my forehead reddened by its crumpled imprint. It is the chapter on the Gupta Dynasty.

Two large bamboo tripods have been set up in the middle of the street, and a tight rope has been strung between them. A woman with hair like a bonfire burning downwards beats a drum with manic preoccupation. I peek in through the balcony window to see if mom has seen me sneak out. A little girl bends herself in half like a slab of Wrigley's chewing gum, and squeezes her body through a metal ring that a little boy holds up. Once through it, she squeezes herself back again, this way and that, over and over, till she seems like that gum has been chewed fully.

The two kids then arch their bodies backwards, hold each other's ankles, form a ring, and roll around like a bicycle wheel. A third child of about six walks the tightrope nonchalantly, as if she is chasing a butterfly in the park. The pyre-haired mother goes around the gathered crowd, collecting money. When she stops below our balcony and looks up at me, I freeze. I can't not pay them something. But if I go in and ask mom for two rupees, she'll know I haven't been studying. I turn away, red around the ears, and run inside. My heart is beating really fast. I am going to study now, I tell myself.

I am going to study really hard.

Four

In the afternoon, I am eleven.

Dad is sprawled on his back across mom and dad's double bed, the *Statesman* held up open in his hands. The late-afternoon sun has drawn the shadowed pattern of the window grill on the white bed sheet. His spectacles have slid so gradually down to the tip of his nose that he hasn't realized it. The newspaper slowly collapses onto his chest. The soft snore that whistles through the mini caves of his nostrils makes for a haunting background score. His left leg is a miniature mountain, folded at the knee peak. His right leg, lifted up, bent sidewards at the knee, is a stone bridge across it. The first two fingers of my small right hand are Tintin, walking across the Tibet snow.

Tintin scales the sheer cliff face of dad's left shin, slides down the raggedy incline to his jagged hip and starts the treacherous trek across the light-blue cotton waist-land. When Tintin has passed the twin howling wind tunnels, and leapt over the fences of convex glass, the ground beneath his feet twitches, and a sudden sneeze makes him disappear.

The landscape mumbles, turns over to its side and goes still again. As the howling in the tunnels slowly returns, Tintin emerges from the thick foliage of black-and-white hair where he had hidden himself. With slow careful steps, he walks around the right ear and prepares himself for another lethal ascent, from neck to the right shoulder. 'This is it, Tintin,' he tells himself, 'it's do or die.' But just then, my eyes fall on the *Statesman*'s comics' page.

Dad becomes a jungle. My fingers, Phantom.

Five

At dusk, I am thirteen.

We have just seen the sun dissolve like Disprin into the Godavari. As the Coromandel Express slows down at Rajahmundry, dad is already up on his feet, combing his hair, swaying gently, as our bogie – the last one in the train – lurches. He picks up our nearly empty Milton water jug and gets in line behind the passengers fidgeting to get off. 'Don't go outside the station looking for freshly made medu vadas please,' mom tells him, 'I'm not going to pull the chain for you.' He smiles, tells her not to worry, and disappears.

When the engine whistles and the train starts to move, he is nowhere in sight. Mom panics.

Five long minutes later, he appears, grinning sheepishly. He plonks the chilled water jug down and tells mom that he had to jump into the first bogie and walk back here through the train. In his right hand is a hot newspaper parcel.

The medu vada melts in my mouth like candy floss.

Six

Late at night, I am sixteen.

I write the labels.

'Bharati Pickles'.

On some bottles I follow that with 'Mango', and on some with 'Mixed Vegetable'. On the lid of each, with a large red felt pen I write 'Rs 15'.

Dad tries to scrub the branded stickers off the empty jam and pickle jars that he had bought from the raddiwallah today. He doesn't do a very good job of it. Mom asks him to soak them in water, saying that she'll take care of it. He keeps a large plastic drum to fill below the bathroom tap and goes back to his *Reader's Digest*.

Mom sits on her high wooden stool and scoops pickle from a large red bucket into a labelled jar, weighing it on the small weighing scale before screwing its lid on. She falls short of jar-lid labels. I say that the red felt pen had dried up, and snap open didi's walkman to flip the cassette over. Okay, she says, and tells me to go sleep. I leave the table, humming.

She looks at the dining table before her.

Forty empty jars.

Four large bowls of marinated raw mangoes.

Twenty iron weighing ingots. Of different denominations.

Sheaves of paper. Coloured pens. Spoons. Ladles. Knives. Bottles of oil. Steel boxes containing spices.

Two pairs of spectacles.

Plastic buckets with pickles.

Her wedding ring, which she takes off each night when she makes pickle.

And her medicines.

'It must be 1 a.m.,' she thinks to herself. 'He will need thirty bottles to supply to the four grocers at seven in the morning. I've packed ten. Twenty to go. The felt pen's dried up. I'll use a ball-point pen. The bottles have to be dry. Or the pickle might get fungus in a month. But I still need to wash them.' And she turns for the bathroom where the bottles have been soaked in the drum.

As she passes the basin mirror, she spots a cluster of her bindis stuck to the glass in a corner. It's funny, she thinks as she glances at her reflection, how she hasn't noticed them all these months. She touches a paisley-shaped red-and-gold one, then pries it off. Absent-mindedly, she puts it on her forehead, but it doesn't stick. Its glue has dried. It has left a mark on the mirror. The stain won't rub off with her thumb. 'Mch,' she says to herself, 'I'll have to use some kerosene.'

Seven

At the day's end, I am twenty-three.

Being many things and many ages from many Sundays past.

As the twitch dies in the space between us, it speaks. At first, I can't tell its voice from the gargling mumble of the river. It inches nearer, sits beside me, its head bobbing digitally.

I take the urn from my lap, and undo the thread that holds the muslin clinging around its damp mouth. The breeze flicks the fabric from my fingers. The sound of the river fills my ears. I feel it murmur to the beat of my heart. I want it inside of me, breaking miniature waves on the insides of my chest. I want to be inside it, to float down the Hooghly, be slapped on a stone, slide down, swirl around it, flow again, into another Sunday past.

The pigeon is watching, as if it understands. As if it was there.

Outside my window.

On top of the double-decker bus.

In the balcony.

On the wire that trailed the Coromandel as it drifted through endless rocky red plains.

It must have been.

To be able to speak to me this way of the Sundays that I have occupied.

The ashes are flakes on the skin of the water now.

She is now a photograph.

Many Sundays later *he* will be too.

As will *I*.

My ashes will pepper the river too. This river. Some river. Some Sunday. From some urn. To a different chanting of the same shlokas. But the pigeon ... it will be there, I think.

And it might even speak of Sundays.

The murmuring priest asks me if I know the meaning of the Sanskrit shlokas I have just chanted after him. I say I know what that pigeon said. But the priest doesn't hear me. He murmurs again. His murmur mixes with the murmur of the river. This murmur hurries downstream past the large murmuring iron bridge. It squeezes past hundreds of murmuring feet. It ripples over thousands of murmuring heads. It rolls and tumbles into the million-murmured twinkling of the city. More and more murmurs join in, millions and millions, growing larger and louder and heavier and less coherent, swirling into a big, soundless, rumbling roar, as if the whole world, its pasts, presents, futures, its living and its dead, all coalesced into one big moan, is preparing to lean into my ear and tell me all that I need to know about living...

... that it will end someday.

I turn to the pigeon.

In a sudden burst of feathers, it flies away.

BETWEEN THE LINES

It was the fourth small pencil gash since the last paint job. I pressed my nose against the wall and crossed my eyes to see if he'd made the mark in the right place, struggling to keep my heels from leaving the floor when I stretched. I tried rubbing out the lower marks with my ink eraser but the paint came off.

STILL LIFE

Mom made me a sandwich and cut it up. Hot milk was cooling in a saucer. My Spiderman tiffin box was wrapped in plastic and secured with two criss-crossing rubber bands. Dad had polished my shoes. The laces were the same length on either side. My tie had been ironed. Suddenly dad's scooter thrummed into life downstairs and he honked '*peep-peep-pi-pi-peep*'.

GOING HOME

The last period on Fridays for class 9-B was biology practicals. I got the corner table near the window. It was the most coveted spot since the breeze kept sleep away and we could peek into the ladies' staff room. But I didn't care about either of those things. I wanted to see *the foetus*.

It sat in a jar high up on a shelf above the window where we couldn't reach it.

I could never tell whether it was a girl or a boy.

CONNECTIONS

Jyoti got herself a gas connection today. Three men invaded her home wearing blue overalls with identical large yellow letters embroidered on their chests that made their names immaterial. They couldn't get the regulator to fit properly. Jyoti can't sleep now. She smells gas with every fourth breath and her heart freezes in fear. She imagines the smell though. The same way she imagines the person she wants but cannot touch each night, and chokes a small breath with the fantasy. That, by the way, doesn't help in her battle for sleep either.

Abhijit can make calls but no one can call him. He says it's strange but he's lost the incoming facility. Not possible, I said to him, and secretly envied him for being able to access the world on his own terms. I remember Abhijit as a doped-out shadow in the jagged darkness of the McCann Erickson office, using Photoshop to marry his photograph with that of the girl he had loved for six years. He had a folder full of such pictures that she had never seen. He discovered how to 'hide' a folder on the iMac and used to keep this folder hidden. So well hidden that once he couldn't find it himself. Last month, I heard he married her. It might have been good but I still don't know if she married him back. I don't get definite answers from him because his 'incoming' is on the blink.

Once, during the year that he had slipped out from under advertising's plastic door, he had called me from a six-digit rural phone number, and told me of the fitful sleep that visited him on the farm. He had taken up animal husbandry. Somewhere in between the goat fodder and cow dung he used to sit under an explosion of stars and scribble Bengali verse. The words smelt of fresh earth. In the snatches of breath between the lines I could hear the corn turn their ears as if to hear him more clearly.

A village girl taught him folk songs. He called her 'Kuhu', the sound a koyal makes, he explained, and whistled like one. At night they'd cycle into the tall grass fields. He'd put the cycle up on its stand and pedal furiously to keep the small headlight lit on the dynamo attached to the rear wheel. In the slim shaft of yellow light, she'd dance like a tree spirit to the rhythmic clinking of the cycle chain. In a little while, said Abhijit, the distant crickets and owls would pick up her beat and the shadows of the paddy fields would sway with her. On those nights, his legs never got tired of cycling. His incoming was defunct even then, but he didn't know it.

Soon, his animals died. The floods hit Medinipur with an unforeseen fury that year. Abhijit climbed back into that worn out chair in front of the 'raspberry' iMac, and opened that hidden folder of married pictures. He started to imagine that life he used to imagine before. He'd have a flat near the bypass. The girl he had loved before would probably agree to live with him. At some point they'd find their secret recipe and sign up for a gas connection.

Jyoti takes lots of pictures. They're for her blog, she says, but they could be because she's afraid of forgetting. She photographs her friends, the statues she likes, pretty chairs, the stray migratory heron, even the goat tethered outside the old furniture shop in Jogeshwari. She clicks them with a masked desperation; so she has proof in case they turn their backs on her someday. She'll know for sure that they were hers for at least those few moments she spent framing them.

Jyoti is new to Bombay. Her marriage is now buried under a pile of raddi, like a forgotten headline. Her second surname drags in the dust behind her, still attached to her by a single frail thread. She takes sharp turns sometimes, hoping the thread will snag on something and snap. The city she left is now a closet of memories. The closet is locked, the memories debris, the dust settled.

But she has photographs.

She watches a housefly now in her strange new house and wonders if it can teach her to take wing too. And then she wonders if she's losing her mind. The failed gas connection, the fungus on the damp walls, a defective curtain rod, a bed she got overcharged for, the dying plant outside her window, the irregularity in the Goregaon water supply, her rebelling stomach and the realization that she's alone in the knowledge of all of this make her want to cry. There's solace to be had in tears, I want to tell her, but I know those are mere words, and words cannot hold a hand or run lightly along a bare shoulder leaving a trail of goosebumps.

But then neither can a photograph.

In Calcutta, Abhijit sits before his phone, hoping to be remembered by somebody, anybody. There are voices at the windows and the door but they aren't voices Abhijit recognizes. He wants to hear one that will make him cry. But he can't. He has no 'incoming'.

LOAD-SHEDDING

All the homes till as far as we could see were either pitch-dark or flickering with candlelight. Everyone was outside where it was easier to breathe.

Dad was in his armchair in the balcony, fanning himself with an oval plastic fan. His pocket transistor was tuned to Akashvani. There must have been other transistors in the balconies of the other buildings in the neighbourhood, because they all played the same *Noorjehan* song simultaneously.

THE RACE

I drove the Flaming Ferrari and gave her a choice of the red ambulance or the black fire engine. She cribbed but I started the race.

We ran the cars along window sills, over pillows, up and down the incline of an armchair, took sharp turns around pickle jars and the curves of the balcony grill. My car engine was very loud. I won.

I looked back in triumph and saw her lying in the armchair running the ambulance up and down her tummy. 'It tickles,' she said, and giggled carelessly.

THE TEST

Mom shelled peas. From the small mountain of pods next to her feet I gently tweezed out the greenest, slowest one with my fingers.

My geometry dividers walked with a slight limp. I drew a circle in the mud with them but it didn't connect in the end.

I dropped the worm in the centre and waited to see if it'll find the opening in the chakravyuh.

SOLVING CROSSWORDS

White boxes. Rows of white boxes with letters in them.

And black boxes. With nothing.

Every morning, when the newspaper had been read, reread and made to feel inconsequential, Ma would pick it up and give it another reason to be. She'd open it up to the crossword page, fold it back four times, until just the crossword was visible and leave it on the dining table with a ball point pen for company. In between doing the dishes, cleaning the grain, washing the clothes, drying them, boiling the rice, ironing the clothes, chopping the vegetables, answering the door, getting the house cleaned, cooking the lunch, she'd stop by the folded paper, fill in a word, mull over some options, read the next clue and carry on.

The crossword was her only involved distraction from the oppressive daily-ness of her life.

Now whenever I think about it, I wonder if it was because of the curious similarities they shared. Ever since she got married and had children, her life had been ruled by boxes. By pre-assigned shelves where clothes, utensils and books had to go. By corners where beds, tables and trunks had to be slid in. By bracketed relationships into which boxes of sweets, monthly phone calls and yearly gifts had to be assigned. Everything seemed to be boxed. Defined spaces. Not meant to be vacant. Waiting for the right letter to be placed there. And it was up to her – devoted wife, earnest daughter-in-law and dedicated mother – to fill those boxes with the right choices.

Her life had black boxes too. The ones that played no meaningful role in her crossword, but the ones that would have bent the rules, brought a sparkle of mayhem in her cemetery of systematization.

We spent our childhoods watching her go across and down, box by box, word by word, criss-crossing letters, making words interact, sticking to the white spaces, hesitantly avoiding the blacks.

After returning from school in the late afternoons, I'd crouch at the head of the bed, where she'd lie down for her only hour of respite. I'd watch over her shoulder as she would try to solve the few remaining words. She'd doze off gently, her pen hovering in the air for a long minute or so before her hand crumpled to her side.

That was my favourite time. I'd slip the newspaper out from her other hand, solve the rest of the crossword and leave it right next to her. She'd awake to another round of regimented duty. But now she didn't have a crossword to help tie up the mundane bits of the evening.

She never told me, but I realized much later, how I used to deprive her of the one thing that made her feel less alone.

She *was* those black boxes. And the crossword was the only thing in the world that reminded her that black boxes exist. That those spaces, where nothing needed to be fitted, could still be hers though she never put her pen tip on any of them. Just seeing them on either side of a train of white boxes comforted her. Her own black boxes were out of reach. Far outside our white-tubelit two-room house-box. Somewhere out there in the warm darkness she could never get to. But they were there.

Those black boxes were in the kathak recitals she watched tiredly on Doordarshan late at night. Those black boxes were in the love letters her students slipped into examination papers when she was *that* botany lecturer with waist-length hair. Those black boxes were in her favourite orange-flavoured Cadbury's chocolate bar. And they were in a childhood spent as her bachelor uncle's favourite niece, indulged with Walt Disney and pretty white shoes. Those black boxes were out of reach, yes, but they were there. And it was the crossword that reminded her of that everyday.

I stop at the crossword page in the papers sometimes. But I've never felt the impulse to solve one on my own. I guess Ma, on her way out, made it possible for me to doodle in the black boxes most of the time, so I wouldn't have to try and weave my way across or down the white ones. I do solve a word or two but then I leave it at that. I like incomplete crosswords. They look like a battlefield where the black boxes won.

Most things don't 'fit' in my life. They hang about in the space, shifting around till they find their corners, or they get tired of the shuffle and leave. Work is undefined. Relationships, transient. Mornings turn to nights without sliding through evenings. And sometimes nights peek out from under bed sheets and get blinded by afternoons. Perhaps, the day I solve a crossword in its entirety, my life will sequence itself like a row of neatly boxed letters that actually add up to a whole word. Until then, I'll probably be many letters with infinite possibilities in permutation. Full of promise. And never realized.

Perhaps.

Or, like most of my unsolved crossword boxes, perhaps I really don't have a clue.

Though in such moments, I wish I could just fold the paper to that page and leave it on the dining table for Ma to pass by it. When it's nearly solved, all I'd have to do would be to peek over her sleepy shoulder. And watch the infinite possibilities coalesce into one. Once it's over, it always seems so simple. But once it's over, it's never the same again.

INDICATORS

The indicators on his scooter had been replaced just that morning with new ones that beeped. He used to forget to switch off the ones that didn't, and would sometimes ride his scooter all the way from the centre of the city to the south with his left indicator blinking. Worried he might cause an accident he had soon reverted to his decades-old habit of sticking his arm out when he needed to turn. And now, even though he'd got beeping ones, he still stuck to using his arms as indicators. At least with those you never forget to bring them down once the turn had been taken, he argued. But in his preoccupation with not causing accidental harm to anyone else, he forgot that he was a ripe seventy years on a scooter that was a ripe thirty. He stuck his arm out to turn right across the tram tracks, wobbled into the track groove, and unable to control the handlebar with just one hand, he tipped over and skidded across the road.

It was an indicator.

In six days his arm was in a sling. And his beloved scooter, sold.

Girdhari rides in buses these days. Refusing to submit to the vagaries of the 'bloody cheaters': taxi drivers. As long as he rode his scooter, he used to feel like he had some control over his life. He had a machine that would do his bidding every time he summoned it to life. But now he waits at bus stops. And wishes he could order the bus to turn into his lane and drop him to his doorstep. He smiles at the thought and adds, 'At least the odometer touched 30,000 kilometres.' His Bajaj Super had lived a full life.

She waited at the stove for nearly fifteen minutes till Lakshmi and Rani arrived. Padmavati had been waiting with her. She berated the two of them for having no sympathy for a hungry old woman. They ought to have arrived fifteen minutes ago. And then, giving the three of them a continuous commentary of her procedure, she set about making herself some dosas. She ground the rice into paste with a mortar and pestle, telling Rani, Lakshmi and Padmavati that she doesn't trust 'those machines', they never do exactly what you want them to. She preferred grinding the rice with her own hands. That way, every last grain submitted to your will. And when you showed the dosa who its master was, the dosa too turned out exactly the way you wanted it to.

'Would you like a bite?' she asked the three of them. And they looked at her silently with unmoving beady eyes from the wall. And then she noticed that Lakshmi had lost her tail. 'Good,' she said, 'good, a new one will grow back, but it's good that you don't know it.'

Nagaratna believed that to cherish what you have, you need to lose a lot of what you love. Loss is the greatest indicator to life.

Rani, Lakshmi and Padmavati were her three dearest friends. Traitors all. They died before her. That too within the same monsoon month. On the first of the very next month, these three geckos appeared in her kitchen. And cooking was no more the solitary exercise it used to be.

The small pocket transistor in the bedroom was tuned into Kishore Kumar singing '*Musaafir hoon yaaron*'. In the living room the radio on an old tape recorder played some muffled Rabindra Sangeet. The dark dining room gently jangled to the voice of Cliff Richards. It was Sunday. The day he stayed home. The day when the only voices he'd hear would be unintelligible static from neighbouring homes or these voices from the past, fossilized forever in public broadcast. So he tuned in to as many and as much as he could. And in the linguistic and melodic cacophony, he fell into a sound sleep.

The music was punctured often though with the RJ's natter and desperately voiced advertisements. When the breaks in music coincided on all three radios, it sometimes woke him up. 'Right,' he'd mutter to himself, as if someone had whispered a reminder into his old ears, and he'd slowly turn over to the other side of the creaking double bed. The momentary death of music was an indicator that he had to turn over, or the damaged shoulder he had fallen asleep on would start to ache.

She told the fair-skinned girl in the ad for Fair and Lovely that until she came along TV no one had ever doubted the beauty of their dark skins.

She scolded the newsreader for tumbling over her words. 'I'm listening to you because I want to know things. How will I know them if I can't follow what you say?'

She told Rajinikant that she had stayed a spinster all her life because she was waiting for him, and she giggled till her paper-thin ear lobes shook.

She asked the chief minister to 'sit down and read the

constitution', and if he couldn't, she would, every night, to put him to sleep.

She blushed when an elephant climbed another from behind on Nat Geo, and told them to spare a dying woman a frantic fantasy. And she laughed at her own joke.

And then she turned off the TV, turned to her empty house, to the river that ran outside the window, and listened to the murmuring it made.

The infinity of sounds that television brought into her life was indicative of the silence that otherwise filled it. Nagaratna was thankful for the disparity, and said 'Good, good' to herself.

The word, repeated thus, carried out of the window, down the river, halfway around the country, across a delta and sneaked in through Girdhari's window.

Just then, the lights went out. All three radios plunged into an abrupt silence. His snoring wavered for a moment before dying too. 'Right,' he muttered sleepily, turned onto his back, and blinked slowly into the pitch darkness.

From the road below, the beeping of a scooter's indicator shrieked through the night.

KEEPING IT FRESH

Pia had asked him to pick up the latest issue of *Tehelka* on his way home.

Large, crisp, white, waxy tissue paper sheets were placed in the folds of all new block-printed sarees before they were folded to be packed in his saree shop, so that they retained the stiffness of their shape.

When he got home, he placed the magazine in Pia's hands. It took her a few moments to realize what it was. He had covered it in the same crisp paper sheets, that too doubly, like he used to do to her school exercise books. 'So that it stays *fresh*,' he said with a beaming grin.

Sitting on her bed, packing the *Tehelka* into her knapsack, looking around her, at the house she had grown up in – and the one her father now was the single occupant of for most of the year – Pia realized then that he 'covered' everything.

All his documents, from his medical test reports to little interesting news clippings, had been slipped into small transparent plastic bags, in the hope that perhaps the non-biodegradability of the plastic covering would ensure an eternal life for its contents too. He bought toffees that he popped once in a while, but mostly gave away to neighbours, little kids, friendly shopkeepers, anyone who was kind enough to ask him how he was doing. Those toffees too – sometimes two or three at a time – had been carefully arranged in little plastic bags fastened by rubber bands. It seemed as if he challenged their expiry dates by packing them up this way.

As she looked around and saw all the covers slipped onto everything in the house, sometimes held in place by elastic, sometimes their mouths tied into knots, she wondered if her dad was afraid of things wearing out just like his memories do.

But then she observed that he put his memories inside little plastic bags too. These were the sealable kind – the transparent slip bags with adhesive flaps. His sarees came in such bags. He emptied them of their intended contents, brought them home, and stuffed them with old photo albums, the licence papers of his now-sold scooter, decades-old receipts, letters, greeting cards, brittle yellowed shop deeds and bills for STD calls made to loved ones aeons ago. Then he sealed these bags and shoved them into the shadowy recesses of the three cupboards that were once shared by the four of them, but which were now available to him alone. He seemed to have filled up all the cupboards' corners with these plastic bags full of memories, content somewhere that neither decay nor age would get to them.

And even if they did, it'd be long after they'd got to him first.

When Pia had walked into the house last week, she couldn't spot the telephone, until it rang. It was hidden under a blue napkin embroidered with pink and green flowers by her mom decades ago. Everything that stood the remotest chance of fading with sunlight or dust had been shrouded in coloured cloth. His two transistors.

The tape recorder. The directory. His plastic biscuit boxes. Little square miniature blankets lay on his strips of medicine. Empty mugs that he'd use to drink tea in the next morning stood on the dining table covered in veils like shy little brides.

Even when her dad finished eating he would immediately cover his empty plate with another, as if unwilling to look at the remains of his meal beneath it.

As Pia leaves him yet again, for Bombay, he gives her her goodbye gift. Not surprisingly, it's a little plastic package. She unties the knot that holds the mouth of the red plastic bag closed, to fish out another plastic bag, a transparent one. Inside it is a thick white crisp envelope fashioned out of his saree packing paper. On unfolding it, she finds a stapled wad of mint-condition ten-rupee notes, worth a thousand rupees. 'Fresh,' he says, 'straight from the bank', to help her in those times when getting change becomes an uphill task. He is a businessman – a shopkeeper – and to his mind, no gift can do more service than something that makes a transaction easier.

And as they disengage from their goodbye hug he reveals to her his ultimate cover, the one that keeps all his sadness, aloneness, his perplexity at his fate hidden from her. He smiles ... broad, beaming ... till it fills up his eyes. Pia's not ready just yet to lift that cover to peek below it. Just like her father, she too doesn't have any answers. But unlike him, she doesn't have any covers to disguise that fact.

Not yet.

And so she turns and walks away, slipping the wad of ten rupee notes back into its dual plastic cover and knotting the mouth closed. Real tight.

'The degree of slowness is directly proportional to the intensity of memory;
the degree of speed is directly proportional to the intensity of forgetting.'

—Milan Kundera, *Slowness*

FORGETTING

He had to pick up the steam iron from the electrician, drop the shop keys off at his brother's house, buy some bread for the next morning, pay the STD shop owner for the call he had made to his son last night, visit the dentist for the final sitting of the root canal and then he had to buy something from the grocer. He couldn't remember what. *By the time the root canal's over, I'll probably remember*, he told himself.

But the professional aloofness of the thirty-year-old woman peering into his mouth made him forget.

His scooter tottered a little when he rode back home. The thought of having to fumble through four identical-looking Godrej locks on his door – always mixing up their keys – tired him as he climbed the stairs.

He sat down an hour later before his dal and rice, half heated, half cold and lumpy, too hungry to care. With the first mouthful he realized he had forgotten to buy a packet of salt. He shut his eyes and did something he had come to master over the last few years. He began to think of this house when it had been full of voices. His wife's, his daughter's and his son's.

The memory distracted him and he quickly shovelled the dal

and rice into his mouth, chewing absently, swallowing carelessly. When he did this, the absence of salt didn't bother him. In this way, in the past five years, he had come to terms with sugarless tea, cold rotis, extra-ripe bananas and soggy biscuits.

As long as he held on to the past, the present seemed to take care of itself.

When he had wiped his plate clean, he opened his eyes. *Salt*, he told himself a few times, *I have to remember the salt.*

PHOTOGRAPHS

There was a heart-shaped window in the lid, covered with cellophane. Whenever a man used to buy his woman a saree, he'd ask for it to be packed in this box, reminisced Magan. There was a huge mirror in Magan's shop wall. It had seen more women draped in sarees than he had. He couldn't match the mirror's tally even if he had wanted to. His cataract had made sure of that.

So he spent this last day in his shop thinking about sarees.

Sarees with memories of marriage bunched into their folds.

Sarees with shuffled silk conversations sealed into their creases.

Those silent, embroidered whispers shimmying through chiffon, like unseen fish in a pond of weaves.

Uncontrollable long tongues of fabric, stoking the endless narcissistic desires of all those happily helpless women.

Soft six-yard streams flooding the shop counters, arrested mid-flow around their fleshy changing curves.

'Now there's that blurred mirror,' thought Magan, and it told him that he forgot to shave this morning.

Magan looked at the box in his hands. He brought it up, close to his eyes. The stained cellophane heart bore a warped reflection of his face. Through this window he looked into the box, at the small blurred stacks of square black-and-white photographs. These were all that remained of sixty years of this saree emporium. Their thin white borders had yellowed like his old teeth. He knew these memories were useless to him. His eyes would never let him get a clear look at the past any more. But he liked holding on to something.

He tucked the box under his arm, turned to look at the shop one last time. Magan wanted to say something then, but he checked himself.

'I wonder who knocks the heads off mannequins?' he mumbled as he struggled to pull the shutter down, 'I could've done with another face around here.'

WHITE SHEETS

'There's something antiseptic about a white sheet,' thinks Raghu. 'When spread flat, its wrinkles ironed out, it seems so non-judgemental, like it could make anyone or anything pure simply by wrapping itself around them.'

Raghu has no memory of the moment of his birth. But having seen other babies being born, he has made himself a borrowed memory of being wrapped up in a white sheet as a newborn, its edges tucked in under his small chin. In this borrowed memory he remembers feeling safe, warm and peaceful, looking up in wonder at the people of the world he was to inhabit. The white sheet was his first protective cocoon outside of his mother's womb.

Every Thursday, Badi-mamma, his grandmother, would hold a holy satsang at their place. She'd sing shabad hymns for a gathering of middle-aged to old women. Before the satsang began, several folded white sheets would emerge. Raghu and his little sister Munmun had been given the duty of holding the sheets at either end, stretching them creaseless and placing them on the floor, edge to edge, covering every inch. By the time the old ladies arrived, the floor would become a flat cotton landscape of white. For those two hours each week, the house felt pure, sanitized of sin.

Their mother had relinquished her hobbies to be a good parent to her two children. She had one fetish though. She collected printed bed sheets. No bed sheet was allowed to stay on any bed for more than a fortnight. And they were used in rotation, so they'd never fade or lose the elasticity of fabric. As a rule, Raghu and Munmun had to take off the coloured sheet before they slept at night and replace it with a white one. Sleep was comfortable when buoyed by white. Over his childhood then, Raghu came to associate white sheets with sleep.

In time the coloured sheets did fade. All the care their mother took of them served only to delay their demise but they didn't last. It was Raghu's first tryst with the inevitability of death when he saw his mom's prized bed sheets being tied up in a bundle one day. He had sat behind his father on their scooter, the bundle pressed between his chest and his dad's back, his arms barely circling its ample girth. And they had taken it to the Missionaries of Charity in Kalighat where his dad had made him hand it over to the sister-in-charge to be distributed amongst the poor. Raghu remembers noting how the sisters there wore white sheets for sarees, the whiteness bordered by a single blue line.

When Raghu came home that day, night had fallen, and he had to change the new colour sheets that his mom had spread on the beds, for white ones, before sleeping. The white sheets were the same old ones. 'White,' Raghu realized that day, 'doesn't fade.' In fact, the sheets had become softer, more comfortable to sleep on, aware of every contour of their bodies, in tune with every toss and turn, flapping with the breeze of the ceiling fan to the faint rhythm of some white lullaby.

The white sheets had appeared to be winning the wrestling match against time.

Many years later, their mom started to fade too. She had battled the pain that plagued her for years, the same way she had battled for her colour bed sheets. Now every hospital bed she occupied was covered with a white sheet. She took a walk in the hospital corridors every evening to strengthen her legs. One evening, Munmun had cut some papaya into small pieces for her … the red variety, sweeter and juicier than the others. One piece had slipped off the fork and dropped on her bed. Raghu had soaked the juice off with a paper napkin but a faint orange stain had remained. When they returned from the walk, the stain was gone. The sheet had been replaced. The bed was virgin white again. Raghu remembers his mother standing there, looking at it for a long time. That evening, the whiteness of that white sheet hadn't seemed inviting. Instead, it was cold, not in a soft snow kind of way, but like a hard smooth block of ice.

This morning Raghu's mom took her last breath. His kaka asked him to help carry her off the bed onto a crisp white sheet spread out on the floor. Around the sheet the mourners sat. It looked like a satsang, thought Raghu, though it wasn't Thursday. His mom looked pure and safe and peaceful. She was sleeping just like she always did, on a white sheet. Raghu had wanted to wrap it around her, tuck it in under her chin, but it wasn't big enough. As the morning progressed, several stains had started to dot its whiteness.

'If she opens her eyes now,' thinks Raghu, 'the first thing she'll do will be to get up off the sheet, bundle it up and soak it in warm water and detergent. I bet she'll add a capful of Robin Blue to ensure the sheet's original whiteness returns.

'But what if it doesn't?'

UNTREATED

Paint peeled off the walls in a hundred dry wounds, the pale scabs flaking to reveal the pink flesh of plaster beneath. This ageing paint was all that was left of the colour of his wife's favourite saree. He had given it to an ashram when she passed away, knotted up with many others. Knotted, like his heart felt some nights when the peeling paint reminded him of her skin.

It had started peeling too in her last weeks. The ointments hadn't helped. So many tubes were left behind, long past their expiry dates, of no use to any ashram.

Unlike her sarees.

He wondered now if he should apply the ointment on these walls. Scabs are scabs, he told himself, whether on skin, wall or memory.

With that thought, he turned away from the wall, rolled onto the other side of the bed, where another memory lay, its wounds untreated, as if daring him to get over it.

THE FIRST BITE

By chemo 9, I couldn't swallow. So he stayed on a liquid diet too.

He cremated me today.

On his way home, he stopped to buy a samosa.

I can't tell if it's the spice that's making him cry.

THE INITIATION

I threw a flat pebble across the water. It bounced once and went under with a *plunk*.

Dad said that a man dives to the bottom everyday and collects the stones that people throw into the pond, and places them back on the pathway where people pick them up from.

He shelled some peanuts and dropped them in my hand.

I thought of the stone sinking.

On the next bench, a couple, eclipsed by a black umbrella, stole a kiss and giggled.

NINE CONVERSATIONS

One

'I like chopping onions,' she said, 'because it makes me cry. But then I start bawling, and the food ends up tasting saltier than it should.'

Two

'My heart feels heavy today,' she said on sms.

'Hearts are heartless things,' he typed, with a ☺.

'Not funny,' she texted back.

'It's the luna again,' he typed. 'The sea today looks like it could devour a thousand Ganeshas, swallow a million dead bodies, wash away an entire city, and not regret it.'

Three

'How heavy is the rain there?' she asked.

'Close your eyes,' he said, 'and imagine a thousand whispers going "sshhh" simultaneously.'

Four

'We just met the lawyer,' she said, 'to start processing the divorce papers. We were like two schoolkids, laughing nervously, filling in each other's words.'

'Sounds like a first date,' he said.

Five

'I'm all alone,' she said. 'And I just rolled my first joint all by myself. It looks like a baseball bat.'

Six

"Thirteen words to comfort, give me ☹,' she texted.

He typed, 'When. You. Wake. Up. Tomorrow. Everything. Will. Be. Just. The. Same. Yet. Different.'

Seven

'There's a pigeon outside my window,' she said softly over the phone, 'it comes and sits there every night, and peers at me.'

'You know what they say about pigeons that don't go away?' he asked.

'I don't want to know D,' she said quite firmly, 'I have trouble sleeping alone.'

'You need to get over your fear,' he said, 'and it's a beautiful thought.'

'Don't say it, or I'll hang up.'

'They are the departed souls,' he said, 'that need to get in touch with the living.'

<click>

Eight

'I'll leave you my clay birds in my will,' she said.

'Can I set them free?' he asked.

She paused.

Then she said, 'You just did.'

Nine

'Two people are like two globes,' he said on sms. 'When they touch, they touch only at a single point. And while these points remain in contact, all the other points await their turn.'

'So what point do you think we've touched at?' she asked.

'Nosetip,' he said.

BEAUTIFUL PEOPLE

The club was called Someplace Else.

A beer bottle had been smashed right outside the door. I stood there watching it being cleared, waiting to go out. She stood on the other side waiting to come in.

There was a cut above her lip, but in the low neon light it looked pretty.

Her watch showed the wrong time.

LETTING GO

She had finally allowed me to kiss her.

'Anywhere,' she had said, 'but not on my lips.'

We stood awkwardly at the ninth-floor window and I touched her like a gawkish schoolboy.

I left to get her some water. I paused at the door and looked back at her sharp silhouette against the street light. I brought her a bottle but she didn't drink any.

She wanted it chilled.

EQUESTRIAN

The orange in the wings licked up in flames as if consuming the green near the tips. The one next to it looked like a pair of painted eyes from some freakish masquerade. They were a row of pretty blotches. She had lain them single file down the centre of her bed. We lay quietly on either side, looking at the procession.

Playing with her nails, she asked, 'What's the craziest thing you've ever done?'

I thought real hard.

'I *came* while riding a horse once,' she murmured, and looked right at me.

The phone rang.

I said, 'Hello? Oh, we're in bed with butterflies between us.'

JUGALBANDI

By four in the morning we had been on the phone for three-and-a-half hours.

She was naked, painting with one hand and holding the phone to her ear with the other. I heard her scraping the canvas from time to time.

My phone was cradled in my shoulder.

Six pages into my writing, my pencil tip broke. I was sharpening it now, softly, so as not to disturb the sanctity of our silence. But not too soft, so she'd know that I was still there without having to ask me.

CARBORISED

Her legs swung outside the window. She perched lightly on the railing and said, 'I like having nothing to hide,' and struck a match to light her cigarette.

'Sometimes when you have nothing to hide, you might have nothing to say.' Having framed the sentence inside my head, I was about to say it, when she held the matchbox up to me and turned it over.

Behind it, a legend read, 'Strike gently, away from body.'

FOREST FIRE

'I'm dying,' she moaned.

'In the jungle,' he said, 'only the rhinoceros runs towards a fire to stamp it out.'

And he lowered his horn to charge her.

BREACH

You touch my skin. A riot breaks out inside of me.
    Shutters drop.
    Sirens wail.
    My eyes call a curfew.
    Still, you climb my fence …
    … and get shot on sight.

DISENGAGED

He said he'd given his ring to a goldsmith to melt and make into a medallion.

She looked at her own naked finger, when the sky rumbled. She got up to take the drying clothes off the clothes line before it began to rain.

As she threw the clothes on the bed one by one, she asked him to fold them 'neatly, so they don't need to be ironed later'.

'Om,' he said, the medallion would be an Om.

'Those who know aren't up to those who love;
nor those who love, to those who delight in'

—Ezra Pound, *Confucian Analects*, 6.XVIII.1

THE RIDE

Three feet behind him is a woman he just met this evening. At the party she had switched his glass with the narcissus's sitting next to her so that narcissus would have to go around the table to get his, while Deep could go sit in narcissus's seat, next to her. She has just told Deep that his nipples are showing through his drenched white shirt. He wants to touch her now, but she laughs. The sand is shifting dramatically under his feet as the sea waves lash and recede. Something blurs his sight. It may not be the rain.

Much further behind him is a woman, not on this beach, whom he wanted to marry, but she decided they had never wanted the same things, so it would not be right for either of them. These days she meets prospective husbands on blind dates. She does not take Deep's calls. She misses him as a friend, he knows it. But that's just a pointless bit of trivia.

There was a monsoon not very long ago when Deep had sat with her at her window near the sea and watched the sky fill up with chalky grey clouds. Her long hair had whipped his face in the strong breeze. She didn't realize it, and Deep never complained. The ends of her hair stung his face gently like the uncertain drops of first rain. Those clouds that evening, though filled with promise, never precipitated. She felt cheated. But Deep was smiling. He had had his little downpour and laid his head on her sloping shoulder, satiated. But he didn't feel her shoulder slacken to welcome the weight.

They clearly did not want the same things.

The woman standing three feet behind Deep is dressed in red. The kind of red that blows up like an upturned flower in a breeze. Her legs, revealed thus, scissor the soaked darkness of this night. 'Normally,' thinks Deep to himself, 'I like being cut, but tonight—' he hesitates. A voice he doesn't remember well from the past had told him once that this woman is married. She loves her husband. It's the kind of love Deep understands but cannot see. It must be the blur in his vision, which may or may not be the rain.

She mistook him for a waiter at the diner where the party was. He was dressed in a white shirt dangerously similar to those worn by the employees there. He offered to bring her her drink for a winsome tip. Much later in the evening, obliviously ensconced in the centre of a room, that seemed to them like a corner, they exchanged notes about their lives. She loved the mountains, she said. She loved not being aware of her individuality at twelve thousand feet.

'The mountains make you surrender yourself to them,' she had said, and dipped her finger in her whiskey. Deep had watched her speak, her eyes sparkling like the dancing tips of a bonfire. He felt the same way about mountains. He remembered how he used to feel up there, like his flesh was carved of the rock, like the rhododendrons were growing out of his own skin. 'Up there, where a lie made as much difference as the truth, I was not me, yet I was most alive,' he had said. That's when he got his tip. She had leaned over and planted the warmest kiss Deep had ever received on his cheek. It bloomed like a rhododendron.

Suddenly the monsoons had returned.

They are two hazy dots now on a soulless Bombay shore. Unlike the mountains, the sea slaps Deep into remembering who he is. His cheeks are flushed. He doesn't know if it's from the slaps, or from all the things he feels and keeps corked tight within himself.

Before him is a raging blanket of grey. White creases form as something under it turns. For a moment he wants to crawl in under this giant blanket and go to sleep. 'If I am asleep,' he thinks, 'these moments, past and present, crashing into me like the swell of waves, might sink into a dream.' For a moment, the sand being sucked out by the receding tide from beneath his feet makes him stumble. For a moment he turns to look at her. She smiles at him and holds up an old battered helmet she has found in the sand.

'Ride with me?' she asks, and some sand pours out of it and forms a miniature mountain between her feet.

THE CUP

'Say something ... something that would sit in a corner as I fall asleep.'

I didn't know what to say.

She fell asleep anyway.

She had a way of saying things that wouldn't allow any more words to follow them in the space they occupied.

One morning, they were standing in her kitchen, the floor of which was sliced in two by a bright knife of morning sunlight. The tea boiled for two silent minutes. It was still boiling when she said, 'Nice of you to drop by.' He seemed mildly offended. He said, 'Gaps in a conversation have a right to exist. All of them don't need to be killed.' A black ant was wandering around his cup. She watched him watch her. Unable to tell him, she leaned over and blew the ant away.

Tonight she wanted to be heard. Perhaps, she wanted to be held too. She didn't know how to ask him. It might kill another sacred gap in their conversation. So she found a cup, made it sit in a corner, waited for an ant to amble by and climb its ceramic side. And watching it walk along its circular rim, she fell asleep.

KITES

'With all those hundreds of kites in the sky, how do you know which one is yours?'

'My heart's attached to it. I know.'

She wished it could be that simple for her too, and she felt her heart helplessly squeeze.

She was in Ahmedabad during the time of the annual kite festival. Everywhere she went were threads. Some were lying loose on the city floor. Some lazed in circles. Some meandered around bends. Some were taut. At their ends were either kites or people. It seemed to her, for those three days, that all the people of the city were connected by threads. She picked one up and pulled on it to see if it would snap. It cut through her finger instead. Watching the blood ooze out, she smiled. There were still some threads in this world not as fragile as hers.

It also appeared that the people were being flown by their kites and not the other way around. When all those bright colours thrashed about in the sky, the difference between colours was forgotten. It was a happy riot. And all the hearts there beat in a happy cacophony. She felt her own join in the rhythm. She clapped like a baby. And before she knew it she was up amidst the kites.

But she couldn't see whose heart string it was that flew her.

'Her hearing was keener than his.
She heard silences he was unaware of.'

—D.M. Thomas

ATOMS

'You can't tell the speed and position of a neutron both at once,' she said, her voice skidding through the darkness.

'Einstein said that a long time before you did,' I said, and struck a match.

She ignored my remark and continued, 'If we break ourselves down to the bare essentials, we're all neutrons, right?'

I nodded, snorting out some smoke.

'Even though we can't tell where the neutron is going to be, we can watch a spot in its path and wait for the moment when it appears there because we know that at some time it will.'

'And when it does, we'll know what we didn't know all this while,' I added.

'The same applies to a collection of neutrons,' she said half mysteriously. 'Us.'

And as soon as she said that, I suddenly knew where I was.

I had been a newly planted sapling on the road divider, two opposing streams of headlights and tail lights screaming by on either side.

I had been an eroded gravestone, standing sentinel over long-decomposed remains, showered clean by falling red flowers for two months every year.

I had been a bell at the end of a greasy chain outside the temple door, being fondled by a thousand hopeful hands every day, tiring of the solitary sound of my ring.

I had been a semi circular window at a railway ticket counter, forever gaping. I had swallowed and spewed out countless restive hands, fumbling for an excuse to go somewhere.

I had been a traffic signal. I had been three colours. And the world had obeyed my command.

I had been a stone bench by the cobbled edge of the sea, silent bearer of the burden of a million lonelinesses.

I had been a train bogey wheel, scratching against metal, scurrying to distant places to come right back, a regimented roller in an endless stretch of identical discs.

I had been the power-saver forty-watt bulb that threw the same shadows in the same room any time of the day.

I had been the sun, that doesn't.

I had been them all. I had been in all those places. I had been there at all times. I had been speeding through them all, being each by turns, knowing that no one could tell my speed and position both at once, so I could get by.

But suddenly she had pinned me down. I knew now where I was. I was sitting four inches to her left, on the edge of a virgin white terrace top that seemed to bleed out of the blackness of the sky. I was her neutron. She had watched this spot, four inches to her left, waiting for me to appear there, and had looked at me when I did.

And when she looked at me, I froze.

Everything I had been, broke away from me in little

pieces and vaporized into the black. I had been sucked into an elemental little thing. I pulsed, a small centre of all that I thought I was and never knew. And as she watched, I slowly slid into orbit around her.

She turned away, smiled to herself and said, 'You can't tell ... you just can't tell.'

THE ASTRONAUT'S SONG

'The astronaut sings karaoke.
Every night.
With all his might.
But no one listens.'

A friend read this somewhere, imagined himself sitting suspended mid-air inside a shuttle, looking out into the endless black ink outside the porthole, then typed it on his phone and texted it to Neel.

Neel guesses his friend Diggy didn't have the audacity to sing a song in his one-minute fantasy. Diggy's lived alone earlier, thinks Neel. He knows what it feels like to sing a song to the darkness, a song no one will ever hear. Diggy's married now, and though he doesn't realize it fully, he tries to distance himself from that shrivelling sense of loneliness that he's left behind.

Just before Neel's phone glowed with the SMS, Mini had been over. Her parents had left town a couple of days back. It was one of those rare periods when her home was bereft of human voices except for her own. The shadows outside her room door suddenly began to seem organic. When her parents were around those very shadows had been still, cold geometric outlines carved out by tubelight hands. But when she was alone, they moved. Picture frames were ghostly faces. Dull sounds were whispers. The squeaking of the fan was a wail growing louder. She was alone. And worse still, she was alone in the knowledge of what that did to her.

Neel had always had an uncontrollable urge to touch Mini. But a touch, when unexpected but intended, can freeze time and alter familiarity. When she spoke of the strangeness her solitude brought her, Neel wanted to reach out and touch her.

Neel lives alone too, most of the time, in a house with two other rooms, several dark corners, hundreds of silent books and the ghosts of moments past replaying themselves on his couch, his bed and his chair whenever he imagines them.

He wanted to reach out and touch her because a touch can give a very specific context to alone-ness. His alone-ness creeps up to him with the specificity of how the edge of the table looks from where he sees it seated in his chair, of how many times the crow in the tree outside caws within the span of a minute, of the difference in the shade of red when seen by tubelight or bulb.

But when he is touched, these specificities get blurred, and that spot of skin comes alive as if gently scalded.

Neel can't tell if that touch does good or bad, but that touch, from another's fingers, while he is sharply aware of his solitude, makes him feel most alive. As if he knows he is alone, yet not.

Which leads him to think of the astronaut.

Perhaps the astronaut knows that there is no one to listen to him sing. And he is aware of that before and after his song. But while he is singing it, he sings it with all his might, and his words are like someone else's fingertip touching his skin. And while he sings, he is not alone. The shadows, the edges, the glows of far-off suns outside the porthole, all blur. And then return to their specificities when his song ends. No one really listens to his song. But in those few minutes he has been touched.

Perhaps.

Mini left soon after. There was another friend she had to meet. She was trying to delay going back home as much as she could. Neel had felt like touching her then too. A gentle brush of the hand against her cheek. Take her hand in his for a moment perhaps. Or even touch his fingertip to her nose tip, like *E.T.* would do. Something to leave her with the sense of being not-alone. It would blur the sharpness of her solitude that night.

But he couldn't bring himself to. There would be corollaries, interpretations, clinging like bramble to that thought, the possibility of awkwardness. That takes the value of memory out of a touch, injects it with doubt. And that might make her feeling of alone-ness much more acute. He didn't want to risk that.

He just hoped, as she stepped out of his door and jabbed the button for the lift, that she had a song to sing to her darkness tonight. In those few minutes she might blur gravity itself … and float.

And if the night is really quiet, thought Neel, he might even hear her.

'Living and ceasing to live are imaginary solutions.
Existence lies elsewhere.'

—Andre Breton

THE FAG END

This is the noisy kind of window, thought Avni to herself as she tried to latch it. The kind that slides down shut all right but will keep her awake by rattling all night in some tribal rhythm, as if in sync with the clacking of the train wheels. It reminded her of the kicking in her stomach. That kept her awake too. All night. Most nights. It reminded her too of Jishnu's snoring. His snores weren't a dull, monotonous drone, the kind of noise you could fall asleep to if you tried. They were raspy, irregular, the rushing wind hitting speed breakers inside his trachea. She'd told him to stop smoking. But he *needed* it, he said. *He* needed it. He didn't care what the sounds from his corroded respiratory tract did to her sleep cycle. Avni wondered now if she herself needed a smoke, to shut out the racket this noisy kind of window was making.

The brighter yellow lights in the first-class sleeper compartment of the Coromandel Express seemed to have extinguished themselves. The dull blue ones in the aisles had come on, filling the bogie with a strange cloudy glow.

The train had started from Chennai ten hours behind schedule, waiting patiently at platform no. 5, as the upside down carriages of the derailed goods train, two kilometres out, were cleared from its tracks. Most of the harried passengers had been screaming and rushing about, as if creating enough of a ruckus would scare the train into starting itself. But Avni had waited patiently, like she'd done most of her life. What's ten hours in a life spent mostly waiting, she'd thought to herself, and amused herself with the gentle kicking and screaming of the little passenger inside her.

The rattling window shutter kept her awake just like it had promised it would.

The lamp posts speeding by outside the window threw dramatic shadows on the insides of the bogie, emerging near the window wall, shooting angularly across the floor, darting up towards the ceiling, swallowing the upper berth and disappearing, replaced by new ones. They appeared, disappeared, appeared, disappeared, with a hypnotic cadence, slowly pulling Avni's eyelids down over her bloodshot eyes.

But the anxiously stuttering window kept them open. Her half-closed eyes travelled sleepily through the compartment. In the two berths on the other side was a young couple, evidently married just a few days now. The lower berth was empty. They were both squeezed in on the upper one, cocooned inside a single sheet, in a little world all of their own. Until about an hour back, the cocoon kept changing shapes, and hushed moans and whispered confessions slipped out of its small openings every once in a while. Their world had fallen silent now. They must have drifted into a sweet entangled sleep, thought Avni, a sleep they'll remember often in their later years.

Also, the husband didn't snore.

Her back began to ache now, so she turned as far to her side as her bulging tummy would allow, which wasn't too far, but far enough to not awaken the sleeping rattler inside. Half turned to the wall, her eyes fell on the corner of a sheet that had slipped through the crack between the wall and the berth above. That sheet might have been hers, but the man up there now was concerned enough to trade his berth with hers, as she couldn't climb up in her state.

In her state.

Those words make a pregnancy sound like a handicap. Perhaps it is one, thought Avni tiredly. Why else would it be her burden to bear alone? If it truly was a 'joint project' as the architect Jishnu liked to call it, he'd be here right now, helping her with the execution of it.

She'd never asked him his name, the man up in berth no. 22. He seemed to be sleeping quite soundly now. He's either unmarried, she thought, or has made his peace with the institution. With every lurch of the speeding train, his sheet slipped a little lower till its edge touched Avni's stomach. She watched it slip, not really minding how the sheet's tip was now gently tickling her navel. She felt her baby gently turn over inside. Her mind wandered to this man.

He was good-looking, she thought. The kind of good-looking that doesn't make you do a double take in the middle of a crowded platform. But the kind of good-looking when lingered over for hours soaks into your heart like ink on blotting paper, leaving behind an indelible smudge. How unattractive she might have seemed, with her bulging stomach and the bags under her eyes.

The top three buttons of his shirt were undone. She had found it interesting that a man of such few words, so private that he almost seemed cold, would wear his clothes in such a manner of warm invitation. He'd caught her looking at him once or twice and looked away quite matter-of-factly so that his discovery wouldn't discomfort her. The one conversation she had tried to start, about swapping berths, had derailed as soon as it had been begun. He'd already thought of it, seeing her 'state', and swung his only bag – a tote bag – onto the top berth, and slid her suitcase under this seat. It was a very heavy suitcase. But he grabbed it, lifted it right off the ground, and slid it under with such surety and speed that it made her feel safe.

Strange, thought Avni, that a complete stranger, through a completely innocuous act, should make her feel that. *Safe*. As if the world, up until then, had made it a habit to make her feel pervious to its inconsistencies. That made Avni wonder how calm he must look now, sleeping.

Suddenly the sheet got pulled up. And Avni's gut went a little cold, the kind of cold she'd last felt when she was caught cheating in a spelling test in fifth grade.

Watch it Avni, she scolded herself, you're going to be a mom now. And with that, she forced her mind away from no. 22—it creaked now as he turned over—and back to the rattling window.

The morning brought Andhra, and the plains were hot. The train seemed to slow down every few minutes to catch its breath, and then would start its metallic galloping again. Avni had changed into her nightie. It was cooler. And roomier. But, she thought – standing clumsily in the bathroom, the nightie over her head, her arms still to pass through it – that it made her look even more unattractive. She had stood there, her feet far apart, trying to stabilize herself against the mindless swaying of the train, and had worn the cotton nightie anyway, allowing her head to finally win the argument.

The little thing inside her was quite a guzzler. Avni wished she knew whether to refer to it as 'him' or 'her'. It might've made her anal preoccupation with pronoun propriety a little more bearable. But that was not to be. Nobody said having a baby was easy. Struggling with pronouns is the least of it. Wait till he ... till it, or whatever, comes out of her, she told herself, that's when the real marathon begins. The race that never finishes. The race where you remind yourself every minute that you're still running it, that the finish line is somewhere beyond the horizon. The race, though, where you can stop to drink if you're thirsty. Which brought her rambling mind back to her water jug. It was empty. She, rather her baby, had been drinking water all morning as if storing it for some future life. So that, perhaps, it'd never need to drink any, once it slipped out into this world. She tilted the jug and poured the last of it out into its plastic cap. As she emptied it into her mouth, the train started to slow down. She pressed her face against the bars of the window, trying to see if a station approached.

'Would you like me to get that filled for you?'

She looked up, to see no. 22. He had climbed down from his bunk and was standing in his pyjamas, running his hands through his tousled hair. Damn the nightie, she thought, and smiled as she held the jug out for him.

The couple was still asleep, oblivious to the heat baking the universe outside their little world. No. 22 sat beside Avni now, disinterestedly eating a large omelette with some bread and butter out of a newspaper sheet. 'How's the omelette?' asked Avni, peeling herself a banana. 'Tastes like one,' he said, 'I've had worse. I would have offered you a bite but I don't think you would've taken it in your state.'

'No,' said Avni dryly, 'not in my state.' And she stuffed the banana into her mouth to obstruct any further words from leaping out.

She held on to the banana peels for a while, watching the trees run by her window, and was about to toss them out of the window when he offered to throw them for her. He collected her peels into the newspaper ball in his hands. She watched him go as her bloated belly lurched. 'What?' she asked her tummy, 'still hungry?' and took a deep breath to calm the little one down.

They sat in silence for a long time. He pored over some pages of the newspaper, completely ignored some others. There was a queer decisive manner about him, like he knew which bits were useful to him, and which were dispensable. He didn't so much as peek at the pages he skipped, looking away at the window as he flipped them. When he was done with it, he asked if she'd like to read it. She didn't. So he got up, left, and when he returned, the newspaper wasn't on him.

The flatlands outside had given way to a rocky landscape. The train appeared to be worming its way through the plateau. Every once in a while, dark red walls would rise on either side and the train's metal clapping would rise with them in an echoed chorus. The sound drowned all the thoughts that were swimming inside Avni's head, so that when the red walls fell away again, her mind was a blank chamber. She turned to no. 22 and said, 'I didn't get your name?'

He instinctively offered his hand, as if startled into doing so, and said, 'Saahil.'

She took his hand and noted how firm yet reluctant his grip was. 'You're Avni,' he said just as she was about to say it. Okay, thought Avni to herself, he just rallied me right back. 'How did you—,' she asked clumsily.

'The reservation chart outside,' smiled Saahil shyly, 'there was you and Mr and Mrs Dwivedi up there.' He pointed at berth no. 24, the little white cotton planet, still balled up, still in orbit. Avni smiled. 'Yeah,' she said, 'they are a pretty enthusiastic couple.'

'They all are in the beginning,' said Saahil.

Something went 'crash!' inside Avni's head, the tips of her ears smarting as if bitten by the jagged teeth of that truth.

'You're married?' asked Avni, uncertain if it was a good idea to ask him that. That question plays strange tricks on those that are asked it, and on the ones that ask. It's a question that's heavy with suggestion, yet perfunctorily light. As much as it could be an invitation, it could also be the slamming shut of a door. It could be well-meaning curiosity – a preamble to a scroll of advice – or it could be the beginnings of a diatribe on those that are not. Married, that is. Saahil rallied again. 'What do you think?' he asked her and smiled. There was no naughty glint in his eye, nor was there the smug twitch of a challenge thrown. He just asked it and waited as Avni looked into his eyes as if searching for the same things that defined her as married. She couldn't tell. He saw that and said, 'I am.'

'Damn,' said Avni, 'I've never not been able to tell before.'

'Aren't you going to ask me to guess if you are?' he smiled.

'No,' she said, laughing nervously. His self-assuredness had made little butterflies take wing inside her stomach. Or no, wait, that must have been her baby. It's easy to mistake that sensation for a butterfly. I'm sure it's even the same size as one, thought Avni. 'How many months is it now?' asked Saahil.

'Seven,' said Avni, looking down at her stomach out of the

sheer habit of doing so every time the topic came up. 'And it still hasn't sunk in.'

'It will when the baby's out I guess.'

'Or maybe not. We – I didn't plan this.'

'Oh,' muttered Saahil, caught unawares by the excess of information.

Just then berth no. 24 creaked and a head emerged from under the sheet. 'Hi,' said what-must-certainly-have-been Mr Dwivedi. 'Good – er –' and he looked around to make sure, '– morning … have we passed Vijaywada?'

'No, not yet,' said Saahil, I think we'll only get there by about eight at night.'

'Oh,' said Mr Dwivedi, startled, and ducked under the sheet again for a hastily muttered conference with what-must-certainly-have-been Mrs Dwivedi. A few moments later his head popped out again and he said, 'Sorry to bother you, but could you let us know when the train stops at some station around lunchtime?'

'Visakhapatnam. About two, I think,' said Saahil, 'I'll let you know, Mr Dwivedi.'

'Uh?' he said, surprised at the unexpected familiarity, mumbled 'thanks', and quickly disappeared into the sheet, unwilling to spend another moment in the outside world. The Dwivedis' low mutterings from within the sheet continued for a while, and were gradually engulfed by the cacophonic chorus of constant train sounds.

Light fingers of breeze gently whipped into Avni's face at the window, massaging her eyelids, coaxing them shut. From far away, Avni thought she heard Saahil say something. Her eyes opened to find him there, a couple of feet from her face, looking concerned. 'You should lie down, I'll go back up,' he said.

'No, no, please ... sit. This thing,' she said pointing at her belly, 'will never let me sleep lying down. It's better this way. The breeze is like a lullaby.'

'Do you write poetry or something?' asked Saahil, sitting down again. '"A breeze like a lullaby" ... you should write that down.'

A sad smile, of things lost, yet held in fond memory, flooded Avni's face. 'I used to write everything down. Colours of landscapes. The difference in the way railways' tea and railways' coffee singed the tongue. Conversations with strangers on trains. Their names, and what they mean,' she said and looked at him. 'I used to be a travel writer. I've even been published once in Nat Geo.'

'Natgeo?'

'*National Geographic*? That magazine on nature, animals and things?'

'Oh yes, Nat Geo ... Aziza watches the channel a lot. There's a TV channel too, right?'

'You clearly don't watch much television,' said Avni, amused.

'I don't read much either. Only what's necessary. But you and I have a lot in common,' said Saahil mysteriously.

'Really? Like what? This train compartment?'

'Sort of,' said Saahil, 'travel.'

'You like to travel?' asked Avni, her eyes coming alive like a little boy's at the mention of toffees.

'No, this must be only the second train trip of my life,' said Saahil, 'I don't like being displaced too much.' He paused, looking intently at his hands, as if conducting a small ceremony to exorcise a private demon, and then said, 'I'm a travel agent.'

And then after another pause, 'Or rather *was* a travel agent.'

Avni burst into a small amused chuckle.

'It's funny?' asked Saahil, confused about what should be the appropriate reaction to that – to look offended or to laugh along.

'Yes, sort of,' said Avni, 'you're like a halwaai who eats his own sweets for dessert.'

'Or a tailor who stitches his own sherwani,' added Saahil, and broke into a smile, relieved at having to take the second option.

'But you said *was*.'

'Yes, I'm going to – er, going away from Bangalore to check out new options.'

'Like what?'

'I don't know yet. I have a little address book with the names and numbers of some college friends. Some of them have a few start-up business ideas. Let's see.'

'That's really brave,' said Avni, 'just getting up and leaving what you know to try something new.'

'Brave? No, no, I don't think I'm being brave. There isn't much difference between being brave and not having a choice sometimes,' said Saahil, looking desolately at his hands again, intently tracing his life line, expecting it to throw up some sort of a revelation.

'I wish I could do that. Just walk away from what doesn't work for me any more,' said Avni dramatically, looking at the sprawling rectangular fields outside the window, their lines changing from being perpendicular to her, into oblique slants, as the train hurtled by them, 'go forth and try new things ... or even back to old things.' She turned back to Saahil and said, 'I don't know if you've ever felt it ... how you always wanted your life to be a certain way, and realized that not everyone manages to get there, but you did ... and when you got there you figured it wasn't all that you thought it would be, and then you miss how it used to be, but the change has been made, you willed it, you prayed for it, you made it happen, and now nothing you do can make it un-happen... and I'm rambling.' Avni pursed her lips and gave him a sheepish smile.

'You *can* make it un-happen,' said Saahil softly, lifting his left leg onto the berth so he could face her, warming up to say something that was going to take some pluck. But just then Avni gasped, choked a soft scream. Saahil froze, his ankle grasped in his hand. 'He – it kicked,' smiled Avni helplessly, 'must be thirsty again, the little camel.'

She walked with careful, measured steps, one hand held out on the side, ready to grab a window if the rocking train decided to lurch. Saahil walked in front, backwards, facing her. 'Walking is er, good in this state, I think, no?' said Saahil, unsure if that sounded like patronizing advice or just stupid midwife mumbo-jumbo. 'It's not a state,' said Avni, looking at the floor as she walked, her hand supporting her ballooned stomach from below it.

'I'm sorry. Walking is not good? Then why ... ?'

'No, walking is good, but this – being pregnant – is not a "state" or a "condition", please. I hate it when anyone calls this a "state" I'm in ... I'm not terminally ill ... I'm just carrying a baby.'

'I ... I'm sorry, I didn't mean ...'

'It's not your fault,' smiled Avni, pausing near the end of the aisle, 'everyone says it. I'd like it if you simply referred to me as "pregnant". It puts a lot in perspective. It's direct. It's true. And ... I need to be reminded,' she tapered off.

Saahil caught the look that appeared in Avni's eyes for just a moment, but then he looked away so as to not make her conscious of having involuntarily shared a very private reflection. 'Would you like to stand at the door for a few minutes?' asked Saahil, the beginnings of a faint sparkle in his eyes.

A blanket of wind threw itself at her, wrapping its flow around her body, running cool strong fingers through her hair, filling up her nightie like an air balloon, tickling every pore of her skin, almost knocking her off her feet. Saahil stood at the edge of the doorway, one hand on the handlebar outside, and the other holding the bogie door open. Avni stood a couple of feet inside, holding onto the washbasin, her feet wide apart, rocking gently in the stream of wind as it gushed in at her. At times the wind smelt of old books, toothpaste and neem. She didn't know why, but it reminded her of her grandfather. Her nana had died when she was seven. But the wind seemed to be dissolving those antique smells off Saahil's body right now and carrying them to her. She inhaled, allowing the smells access to her tongue, feeling it flood with a small burst of saliva.

'You're living up to your name,' said Avni, aware of the mystery the statement evoked, and of the exact response it was about to elicit.

'What?'

'Saahil. "The shore". The coast. The edge of the land.'

Saahil laughed a light, childlike laugh. It was exactly the kind of laugh Avni had imagined he'd have, if he did laugh at all – the diametric opposite of the withdrawn but sincere aloofness of the rest of his self. With his laughter his smells intensified.

'And you're Avni . . .'

'The earth.' Avni cut in, 'the land herself. Standing on the inside of the edge.' And she looked at their current relative positioning to make her point. Saahil caught her look, smiled and said, 'You really shouldn't have stopped writing.'

'You're making me want to go back to it,' she said sadly, then quickly recovered. 'This is my first train ride in over five years.'

'You must have been doing it quite often before?' asked Saahil.

'Every week, for years.'

'Why did you stop?'

'I got married.'

'Oh,' said Saahil, feeling instantly stupid for having asked.

'Ticket?' asked a voice from behind them.

As Avni rummaged through her handbag, looking for her ticket, the TTE sat at the end of the berth and ticked their names in the list on his clipboard. He looked at them, pointed at Avni's stomach, and smiling said, 'Chhota Dwivedi?' Avni burst into giggles, still searching for her ticket. Saahil, flustered, quickly shook his head, 'Nahin, sir, Saahil, berth no. 22 … Mr and Mrs Dwivedi—' and he pointed at the upper berth before them. The TTE nodded in realization, not the least bit embarrassed at the gaffe, got up and thumped the side of berth no. 24. Mr Dwivedi's head popped out, alarmed. 'Huh? Is it 2 p.m.?' he mumbled. 'No,' said the TTE, 'it is checking time … ticket,' and he held his hand out.

'You know, I wouldn't have done this otherwise,' said Saahil. They were back at the doorway, a cigarette held clandestinely out of view in Saahil's hand. Avni had positioned herself to shield him from view as he smoked, exhaling into the racing breeze outside. 'I don't know why I even bought this cigarette. I had quit six years ago. As I was about to board the train, this vendor passed by, you know the chaps who have this glass-covered tray sort of thing hanging by a strap around their neck?'

Avni nodded.

'I wanted chewing gum. But when I stopped him, I asked for a Gold Flake instead. I don't know why.'

'Maybe you needed it,' said Avni.

'Maybe,' said Saahil and pointed at the small metal sign screwed into the wall above the washbasin. It read: SMOKING ON INDIAN RAILWAYS PROPERTY IS A PUNISHABLE OFFENCE. Fine – Rs 200.'

'And 200 isn't much for my first smoke in six years.'

'Don't worry, I've done this before, no one will see you,' said Avni.

Saahil looked at her curiously, sucked on the cigarette long and greedily, and let the smoke slowly trail out through his lips.

'Jishnu accompanied me quite often when we were dating. I actually thought he enjoyed train rides as much as I did. He told me later that he hated them, that he accompanied me for my sake. When he told me that, at first I thought it was the sweetest thing anyone ever did for me, to do something you hate only because the one you love enjoys it so much. But over time, it really pissed me off,' said Avni and paused, trying to let go of the thought as soon as she had got hold of it.

'Because what you thought you had in common was actually a lie?' asked Saahil, tapping the ash off the tip of the cigarette into the wind.

Avni looked up, startled, at the stranger who had just barged in through her bedroom door. 'Yes ... yes,' she said, fumbling with the thought as it was thrust back into her unwilling hands. 'After marriage, he'd only want to fly. Apparently, he hated wasting time on a train. I flew along because I felt like I owed him for having come on all those train journeys with me.'

She fell silent.

'All my life I've wanted to be a father to a little girl,' said Saahil.

'So why don't you . . . ?'

'Aziza didn't want it,' he said, and turned to the collection of quiet hills in the far distance. 'I think I'd make a good father,' he muttered to himself and closed his eyes so he could feel the breeze more intimately. Avni noticed his chest again, as the wind whipped his unbuttoned shirt repeatedly as if trying to persuade another button to come undone. Saahil didn't seem remotely conscious of it. Avni wondered if he'd even realize it if the wind ripped the shirt right off him. Should she reach right over and give the desperate breeze a helping hand? This wasn't a good time to be harbouring such a thought, thought Avni, but strangely she didn't feel any guilt or confusion at doing so. She watched the wind grapple with the fourth button on his shirt. She inhaled the wind. She smelt him on it, tinged with Gold Flake smoke. She inhaled deeper. It made her feel a little heady. She rocked gently on her feet allowing the smells to travel through her head, pushing open doors that had been shut for some time now.

Saahil looked at his half-smoked cigarette, lifted his foot, stubbed it against the sole of his shoe and held it out, letting the roaring wind pluck it from his fingers.

'Why'd you do that?' asked Avni.

'If I'd thrown it away still lit, it might have started a fire,' said Saahil.

'No, I meant why'd you not finish it? It was your first cigarette in years . . .'

'Old habit,' said Saahil, with the grave tone of what Avni could have sworn was deep sadness, 'I always kill it before it dies. It gets really bitter at the fag end.'

And he held her look for a long moment, allowing her access to some deeper, intensely personal truth.

Just then Mrs Dwivedi darted by without acknowledging them, her hair ruffled, her skin an embarrassed but radiant pink. Mr Dwivedi shuffled past right behind her, nodded a sheepish smile to the two of them and went and stood guard outside the bathroom door, his head lowered, his ears tuned into the sounds within, ready as a knight to plunge in to her rescue if she so much as yelped. Avni pretended to sway on her feet to the lurching of the train and swung back far enough to steal a couple of peeks at the faithfully lovelorn Mr Dwivedi.

Smiling at all the mischievous repartee inside her head, she turned back to Saahil. But Saahil was leaned out of the doorway, gazing intently at the faraway hills, observing their perspectives shift as the train slid in a gentle curve through the flatlands around them.

The Dwivedis were back inside their world in no. 24. Soft chatter poked and bumped around under their white sheet. Saahil was at Avni's window and Avni sat with her back propped against the window on no. 23. The couple had happily relinquished all claim to the extra berth.

'What's your most prized possession?' asked Avni candidly, in between sips sucked in through a straw that shot out of a large green coconut in her hands.

Saahil looked at her with a mixture of wonder, curiosity and doubt, as if the coconut were some crystal ball, and she were sucking in some secret of his with every sip.

'Why do you ask?'

'Just … I was wondering about mine. I think I used to have a few,' she said and touched her hand to her stomach. 'But after the baby comes out, I doubt anything else will mean half as much to me any more.'

'Or …'

'I might be wrong,' Avni completed his thought for him.

Saahil nodded and said, 'A human tribal mask, with tiger stripes … a photo album of pictures from my childhood … and *Tintin in Tibet*.'

'Wow,' exclaimed Avni, genuinely surprised, 'it really was just a metaphoric question. I didn't even expect an answer, but you're pretty specific, haan?'

'I've often thought of what I would take with me if I were to leave,' said Saahil matter-of-factly, shuttering his emotions, so she wouldn't see more than he wanted her to.

'Leave? Leave what?'

'Everything … you know, home, my work, my city … I've never travelled much, but always wondered what it would be like to just get up and leave one day.'

'Just leave? You mean everything? Your office … your household … all the people in your life?'

'Yup. All of that. *Tintin in Tibet* is my favourite comic. You ever read Tintin?'

'When I was little, yes … my father was a huge fan. He still reads them over and over again. It's one of your three most valuable things?'

'It is. It's a wonderful treatise on the voice within. In it, Tintin simply hears his Chinese friend Chang call out to him in a dream. And he follows that voice halfway across the world to find that Chang truly is in trouble and needs his help. Nobody knows how Tintin knew. Herge doesn't explain it either. But he just did. He listened to that voice. And he followed his heart. It's a simple and beautiful fable. Also, Tintin was this manic traveller.'

'Yes, a travel writer almost, no? An international journalist.'

Saahil smiled broadly at the casual insinuation. 'Yes, you are Tintin,' he said, sounding strangely delighted. 'Imagine bumping into Tintin on my first and only proper train ride.'

Avni laughed and instantly felt a little squeeze inside her belly. 'Looks like he got the joke too,' she said, putting her ear close to her stomach, wondering if the baby might have something important to say.

'Or she,' said Saahil.

'Sorry?'

'You said "he" … but it could be a little girl.'

And their eyes locked again. For the first time Saahil noticed just how pretty Avni must have been. Must have *been*. And probably could be too, once the baby had been extricated. A baby in a womb must suck so much of its mother's energy away – her own nourishment, her fluids, her regenerative power. The baby is a parasite. It grows. The mother is drained. The skin under Avni's eyes was sagging. It had been collecting all the nights she'd spent sleepless, one by one. Her shoulders slouched. Her hair was straggly, where once, Saahil thought, it must have been thick and straight, its ends brushing against her slim ivory waist. And she had a full mouth, not pouting, but full, with lips that curved up at the ends when she smiled. And she had laugh lines around the ends of those lips. Not used often enough, thought Saahil, and imagined how delicious they must have looked. Must have.

And Avni looked away, slurping the last dregs of the coconut water noisily before trying to get up to get rid of it.

'Give it to me,' said Saahil, and took it from her hands. She didn't say anything, the strangeness from the moments just passed weighing like a lock on the gates to her lips.

The wind was hot now. And it droned into the compartment, sandy and thick. The small fans in the ceiling had slowed down because of the increased viscosity of the air. Their blades went fwup-fwup-fwup like submarine propellers struggling through an oil slick. Another of Saahil's buttons had finally come undone. And it hadn't been the wind's doing. But he shifted about in the seat restlessly now.

'You didn't tell me yours,' said Saahil, impatiently trying to dispel the pregnant silence between them.

Avni looked at him and shook her head in slight incredulity. 'I can't believe you asked me that,' she said.

'Why not?'

'I was just thinking about what I'd say if you asked me about my prized possessions.'

'And?' asked Saahil, looking at her intensely, expecting to find some answer he'd been seeking all his life inside the folds of whatever it was that she was now going to tell him.

Avni looked away, then down at her stomach, then up into his eyes, held his gaze for a moment, and said, 'Nothing.'

Saahil missed a breath then. He tried not to look at her stomach, but his eyes pulled themselves to it. Ball and chain. She could have been anywhere, she could have been anything. I could have touched her if she had willed it, he thought, but now she can never even will it, because of her baby. She's its prisoner.

Avni caught his look, embraced her stomach protectively, folded her legs underneath her, and turned to the window. A sudden gust of wind blew her hair all over her face, wrapping it in a tangled mesh. She didn't attempt to clear it. She closed her eyes, and the mesh got tighter.

Dwivedi's head poked out once, he leaned down low from the berth to peek out of the window. 'We're here,' said Saahil, looking at his hands again, 'Visakhapatnam.' He pronounced each syllable of the name as if it suddenly meant something new to him as he said it.

'God, I'm hungry,' said Dwivedi, smiling sheepishly and turned to his missus, who emerged next to him, her hand lethargically stifling a yawn, her bangles tinkling.

'I've got some puri-aaloo if you like,' said Avni to Saahil, uncomfortable with the cloud of anxious uneasiness that had descended between them.

'Huh?' said Saahil, looking at her blankly, the connection between his mind and his eyes severed. 'Puri-aaloo,' repeated Avni, 'or are you carrying some ghar ka khaana that you'd like to share?' And she smiled warmly.

'Uh, no,' Saahil mustered a weak smile, 'I can't cook.'

'Aziza?'

'No, she doesn't like to cook,' said Saahil, and drifted off… and then came back as quickly. 'I'll go now … uh, get some idli-vada or dosa.'

'Why go? They'll come here no?' asked Avni.

'Yeah …' said Saahil, unsure of what to say any more, 'no, there's this uh – place, just outside the station, they make good dosa.'

'Okay, I guess the train waits long enough here.'

'Twenty-five minutes. Long enough,' said Saahil, 'longest stop on this route.'

'You're quite the travel agent, aren't you?' said Avni with another smile that seemed to have been wasted somehow. 'Could you get me one too?'

'What?' asked Saahil, increasingly distracted.

'A dosa, Saahil,' said Avni, placing her words into the space between them carefully now, syllable by syllable, brick by brick, rebuilding a wall that she had managed to break down just a couple of hours ago, hoping he won't slap on any cement in between the bricks. 'Could you get me a dosa too, please?'

And she reached for her purse.

'Please, don't be silly ... you can buy me chai later? I'll get the dosa,' he said.

He didn't, she thought to herself, he didn't slap the cement in, thank God. She couldn't remember the last time she'd made this sort of a connection with another person, let alone another man, that too a married one. Hell, she probably *never* had. This is the first bloody time. Despite her 'state'—it seemed alright to call this a 'state' now, an incapacitation—she felt young again. She wanted to talk to him, to be in the same space as him, breathe the air he breathed, eat out of his dosa, crush her nose into his chest and smell him ... she felt like telling him everything about herself ... about five years' worth of lonely afternoons spent in the same one room ... about devouring Barbara Cartland romances to fill up the hole inside herself ... about the late-night fights ... about the endless TV shows she loved to hate, but watched anyway ... about getting back on the road ... about all the places she wanted to see ... about all the places she had seen, and wanted to see again, to study what five years must have done to each one of them … about trains, he'd know so much … he could be my travel buddy, thought Avni, someone I'd meet just to travel with … What if it doesn't stop there … what if they cross that line … the line that already had three buttons undone … four now … what would Jishnu think? Did she even care what Jishnu thought any more? Did he care what she thought? Did he even *know* what she thought any more? What about the baby?

The wheels of the slowing train let out a metal wail as the train came to a halt. The Dwivedis scampered down like shy squirrels and disappeared. Saahil looked at his hands, held the left one with the right, squeezed it, then held the right hand with the left, squeezed that, took a deep breath, reached below the berth for his shoes, and as he laced up, he said, 'I don't travel too well,' and smiled weakly at Avni. She didn't know why, but she felt her heart wrench as she said, 'You told me, that you don't like displacement.'

'Yup… Now, dosa,' he said, pointing at the door and got up to leave.

'Hurry back,' said Avni, feeling a growing sense of concern for him, 'I don't want to have to pull the chain for you.'

'No, don't,' said Saahil, visibly alarmed at her suggestion, 'at this stop the engine gets shunted to the other end. From here the train will move in the opposite direction.' He smiled, long and warmly, adding, 'We also lose the diesel engine and get an electric one instead.' He lingered there for a hesitant moment, and then he muttered, 'Yes … I know everything.'

And he was gone.

Avni looked at the empty space where he had been just a moment earlier and smiled. 'Thank God,' she said to herself.

The Dwivedis were back in their nest, eating out of an assortment of newspaper packages, making a happy, riotous mess of their first meal of the day. Avni was at the edge of her seat, peering out at the people passing by on the platform, her eyes searching for Saahil. He must know the exact time of departure, thought Avni, almost frantic by now. He knows everything, he'd said. If he knew that the train would now move in the other direction, then he'd also know *when* it'd start moving that way, right? He must know, thought Avni, in a burst of panic, as the engine let out a set of long, loud, bellowing whistles.

With a dull jerk, the train started moving. The few remaining passengers, adventurous enough to loll about on the platform near the door, clambered in as the train hastened from a walk to a trot. There was still no sign of Saahil.

'He hasn't come back?' asked Mr Dwivedi, his mouth full. Avni looked at him, confused, and silently shook her head. Suddenly the entire train smelt strongly of disinfectant. She scrambled for the door, excusing herself past the young man standing there and leaned out. She scanned the platform as the train broke out of its trot into the beginnings of a gallop.

Dwivedi, concerned, was standing behind her when she turned, his young wife peeking out at them from their berth like a curious bird high up on a tree. 'You should pull the chain,' said Dwivedi. Avni just nodded dumbly.

The TTE looked harried. The stationmaster stood behind him, checking his watch every five seconds, worried it might suddenly jump a whole minute without warning if he didn't keep one eye trained on it. 'We can't keep the train waiting, madam,' said the TTE. 'The Rajdhani is due on this track in ten minutes. All the trains are already delayed because of the accident at Chennai,' added the stationmaster, ready to spew more information if required to make his case. Avni looked from one to the other, and said, 'But he said he'll be coming. It's important for him to reach Calcutta. What if there's been an accident?'

'I understand, madam,' said the TTE, 'but do you even know him? Any address, or phone number? You said he didn't even have a mobile phone. Let the stationmaster take his luggage. The reservation records might have a number. He will be able to get in touch with him. Till then, his luggage will be safe in the cloak room.'

'Yes Mrs … ' said the stationmaster, 'madam, you take my number. Call me, or I will call you when he comes to collect. But now this train has to leave, or we will have to fine you.'

'How much?' asked Avni, feeling stupid, but asking anyhow, all logic having deserted her minutes ago.

'Five thousand rupees,' said the stationmaster, helping himself to Saahil's bag, confident his point must have been made.

Avni lay on her side, the window rattling noisily behind her head, the blue light shining dully like a small electric moon in the dark roof of the bogie. The Dwivedis had got off at Bhubaneswar. She was alone in the cabin now. She cast a blank look at the underside of the berth above her. Berth No. 22. The kicking inside her stomach had been really bad all evening. Unable to get off to fill her water jug at the platform water-cooler, she'd bought herself four bottles of Bisleri. She wished now that she'd never started talking to him. She wished he was still just a number. Just 22. Knowing that he was Saahil, and that she had wanted to touch him, made this so difficult.

Damn it.

This was supposed to be just a train ride back home. Back to Jishnu. Back to all the things she didn't much care for any more, but back to the safety of constancy nonetheless, of not asking questions, of not thinking of the possibilities out there, of hoping, praying, begging that things get better once her baby emerges. Of knowing that there might be little chance of things ever getting better.

She shut her eyes tight, took a deep breath, held her stomach, turned slowly, slipped off the berth, waddled carefully to the iron ladder that led to the berth above, and climbed it. She crawled into the bunk on all fours, gently collapsed onto her side, hugged her stomach tight and started to cry.

'Prerna,' said Avni on the phone, 'please, could you bring me the pages that come out of the printer now?'

Prerna stood before her, chewing gum, as Avni pored over the printed pages. 'Your new travel series proposal?' she asked. 'Yup,' said Avni, 'exploring the different kinds of local foods along the Great Indian Railways.'

'Geez, you'll be living in trains for years if that one comes through,' said Prerna, seeming relieved that it wasn't her holding those sheets.

'I hope so,' said Avni with a grin and swivelled out of her chair.

'Hi dad,' said Avni into her cellphone, 'the network's dicey … I'm on a train, yes,' she smiled, 'just like before, yes,' and she looked out of the window as she spoke, as if searching for something as the train slowed down. The furrows in her forehead changed depth as a large yellow signboard floated into view. It read, 'VISAKHAPATNAM'.

'No dad, there's a nurse with him round the clock. Prerna checks in on him every day. I won't be travelling for another year, don't worry. I'm only writing it now. I'll be in Bangalore by tomorrow morning.' Avni stepped off the train even before it had completely stopped, and walked as fast as she could. 'Can I call you back later, dad? His what? Oh, yeah, I thought of one,' she said into the phone, 'Hello? Hello? Dad?' The network bar had disappeared.

The stationmaster watched as Avni signed the register, paid the dues to the cloak room attendant and picked up the tote bag. 'But you didn't know him,' said the stationmaster, slightly perplexed. 'I said, I didn't know him before the journey,' said Avni, and turned and left with the bag.

As the train started again, she sat on her upper berth with the tote bag, staring at it long and hard, willing it to open by itself. Her limbs felt weak. Her arms throbbed with a dull tingling pain. She wanted to reach him. But if his bag was still here, he clearly didn't want to be reached. She was divorced now, she thought, divorced, free, on her own two feet, a single mother, ready to start over, and here was where she wanted to begin, from this familiar stranger's bag.

And then she did it.

She had come prepared. She slipped out her pliers and cut the zipper open, not bothering with the small Chinese lock that held the zippers together. She ripped the interlock of the zip open and looked in. The first thing that hit her was the smell.

Toothpaste.

Old books.

And neem.

There were two shirts in there, identical to the white one he was wearing that day, but in light blue and mustard yellow. One pair of jeans, light blue again. He was wearing a dark blue one that day. They were the same brand, Pepe, the same fit even. He never wasted time with anything he did not need, she thought, and remembered noting that about the way he read the papers too.

Then she saw an address book, a small, hardback brown diary filled with phone numbers. Something told her that even if she called each and every one of the people listed inside it, it would throw up nothing.

What she saw next made her heart an iron ingot dropped in a river. Her fingers slowly went cold as her hand emerged from the mouth of the bag with a blood-red wooden mask, painted with tiger stripes. The mask was a face frozen in an eternal scream. The next thing that emerged was a photo album. She didn't need to look inside to know the pictures it contained.

She sat there a long time, unmoving, looking at the few things spread out on the berth before her, resisting the urge to smell his shirts. She put her hand into the bag one last time and pulled out a faded, tattered old copy of *Tintin in Tibet*. The now empty bag, relieved of its duty, collapsed to its side. She looked at the book as her phone rang. It was her dad.

'Hi dad,' she answered, her voice quivering as she struggled to keep it steady. 'Saahil,' she said, 'I'm going to call my son Saahil.' And the ends of her lips curved as she succumbed to a feeble smile.

Avni sat at the window, her feet up on the berth, her knees bent. A little metal plate on the compartment wall behind her head read '21'. Her hair was tied neatly. As the wind whipped her face, she wrote into a large notebook pinned to a clipboard resting on her knees.

'*At Visakhapatnam*,' she wrote, '*the engine gets shunted to the other end of the train. From here, the train moves in the opposite direction. The diesel engine gets replaced by an electric one. There's no more smoke then at the fag end.*'

THE NEIGHBOUR'S RECIPE

Punctually at dawn, as the shadows of the boats disappeared under their arched shoulders, the group appeared by the jetty, folded over at their waists and sorted fish. A buzzing huddle of slender feet swarmed all over the golden sand, toe rings glittering in the crisp crimson sunlight. Hundreds of open-mouthed fish were apportioned into mini mountains, which were further quarried, and within minutes smaller mounds appeared near each pair of feet. Baskets hit the sand, throwing up little yellow clouds. As silent pomphrets, salmons and Bombay ducks were slapped, without protest, one on top of the other, the koli fisherwomen shred the misty morning air with their high-pitched chatter. Sickles were tucked into waists, along with the pallus of sarees. Checkered pieces of cloth emerged, fluttering down over hundreds of beady, staring fish eyes, as if shielding them from the increasing harshness of the sun.

Manda tucked the cloth into the edges of her basket, bent over, dug in her heels, fanned her toes, tautened her back and hoisted her basket onto her head. The air buzzed like a hive, vibrating with goodbyes. She turned her back on the sea and started walking towards the bus stop, her hips swishing rhythmically like a fish's tail.

The red double-decker bus negotiated a U-turn in the narrow neck of the lane. The conductor walked along the side of the bus, slapping its metal rear as a farmer would his bull, telling it to reverse. The bus obeyed. And then lumbered up like a gentle throbbing giant alongside the queue that snaked into the Versova Village bus stop. The people ahead of Manda pressed forward urgently to escape the stench of the fish she carried. The ones right behind her hung back. Some noses slowed down their breathing. Some got clipped close by fingers. And some others disappeared into handkerchiefs. Manda breathed in deep and sighed, her full bosom heaving with the act. Someone sneezed.

Manda glided through Andheri market, slithering deftly between vegetable stalls, wading through a river of fruit, disappearing around sharp stall corners, her hips fishtailing. Once in a while, from the corner of her eyes, she noticed men turn their necks at angles unhealthy for their spines to get a better look at her behind as she rippled past.

A string of white gajra buds snaked through a sheet of black glistening hair. A chubby face the colour of tree bark emerged from under it, her kohl-framed eyes knit with concentration. Small mounds of fat around the woman's cheek wobbled as her hands tugged gently at something.

A little girl, the same colour, but infinitely smaller, sat cross-legged before her, having her hair made into plaits. She shuffled impatiently. 'Tch!' said the mother in a spiralling Tamil accent, and thumped her little girl's shoulder with her hand, 'Sit still.'

Just like her mother, the little girl was weaving something too. She echoed the words playfully, 'Tch, sit still!' and hit something before her with mock authority.

At the head of this seated little queue of three was an old woman, a few shades darker than the other two, with earrings that stretched her lobes like chewing gum in an attempt to touch her shoulders. Her white hair was being plaited by the little girl. The grandmother turned around and grinned at the other two, her betel-stained red tongue peeking out from the space between her two remaining front teeth.

Manda's basket landed with a soft tired thump right next to this queer queue. Between them sat a large, lazy heap of saffron and white flowers in a tumbler-shaped basket. The mother glanced up at her and asked, 'Where were you yesterday?' Manda fished out four small planks of wood and began to set up a makeshift altar. 'The boats landed just this morning, Kanta,' she said tiredly and slapped the fish onto the planks in a well-practised flurry. A stone plinth emerged from the base of the basket, and she slid the edge of her sickle back and forth along its side. The little girl cringed at the scratching sound. Manda pressed her thumb to the sickle's edge. Sharp enough, she thought, and put the stone by, folded the checked cloth, patted it to the ground and nestled her bottoms into it.

In the meantime, Kanta eased a lime-green rubber band around the end of the thick black rope of hair in her oily hands, gave its paintbrush tip a flick and said, 'Oi Lakshmi, pass me a gajra.' Little Lakshmi had been distracted the last few minutes by the sight of all those big, juicy fish being laid out in a silver-blue row. Kanta thumped her softly on the shoulder, 'Oi girl

... Gajra ...!' Lakshmi blinked, withdrew one hand from her grandmother's white plait and reached out for the flower heap.

As Kanta clipped the tail of white buds to Lakshmi's hair, four fish slipped off Manda's counter, got chopped into juicy cubes of silver and pink and disappeared into a newspaper shroud. She handed the shopping bag back to a kind-looking man whose moustache poured like a stream down the two sides of his nearly invisible mouth. Winding the long cloth handle around his wrist, he stepped up to Kanta. She had already wrapped some flowers in a large, dry leaf and was running white thread around it, so fast that her hands had become a brown blur around the dull green. She snapped the thread on her teeth and held the package out to him. He took a long whiff, turned to Manda and said, 'That's clever ... fish next to flowers ... kills the stench.' Manda laughed a full-throated laugh like distant Diwali explosions. Kanta looked confused. Being a Tamilian, the nuances of Marathi sometimes ran noiselessly past her. Manda explained, 'He says I sit next to your flowers because my fish stink.' Kanta smiled. It sounded true.

Manda was sipping on a small glass tumbler of chai when someone tapped on her shoulder from behind. She turned to see a small sodden statue of mud standing against the sun. In its face, two lips suddenly parted to disclose a crescent of milk white, nearly making her drop her glass.

'Arre, Sachin! What the hell happened?' The boy poked a finger back into the sky, 'That Ravi ...'

Manda bottomed up on her tea and sprang to her feet, unhitching the pallu of her saree from the waist. She turned to Kanta and said, 'Kanta, could you take care of this for about an hour? Please? I'll just see him home.' Kanta nodded.

Manda bent over her display, bringing the heaps closer together, as if reminding the fish that there was nowhere left to go from here. She said to Kanta, 'Bombay duck . . . fifty for a kilo . . . and this . . .' Kanta cut her short, 'I know re, I've been watching you for years now. . . .' Manda smiled, but glanced back at her wares one more time to make sure, and then left, tying her long hair into a bun. She patted the tidy roll, freed her hand, reached down to grab Sachin's little hand and caught a handful of thin air instead. Alarmed, she turned.

He had fallen a few feet behind, hopping hard with both feet, showering the ground with small wet specks of mud.

Kanta wrapped a fish in newspaper and exchanged it for a fifty-rupee note. She tucked the money into a blind corner inside the basket.

Manda stood near the stairs in the double-decker bus. Next to her, a vertical metal rod grew out of the ground and shot all the way up to the ceiling. Hinged to it with one hand, Sachin swung around it like a door in a storm. With every jerk of the bus he thumped hard against one of the two stair walls, splattering mud every which way.

Manda held out six rupees to the bus conductor and said, 'One full, one half.' He took a long hard look at Sachin and said sternly, 'Full ticket for him today.'

A cloud passed in a curved reflection in a large beady fish eye. Kanta stared at it, transfixed by the juicy fish. From behind her, Lakshmi asked, 'Is that ours?' Kanta pressed a two-rupee coin in her eager little palm and said, 'Go, get me a cutting chai.'

Kanta waited for her girl to disappear from sight. Lakshmi stopped once, looked over her little shoulder. 'Go on,' urged Kanta, 'hurry.' Then Kanta looked about casually. And the luscious fish disappeared. She wrapped it hurriedly in a sheet of newspaper. It was a colour page, the top of which read 'Recipe of the week'. Below the headline was a picture of a fish curry. The folds gobbled up the headline:

Smell something fishy?

She sneaked the parcel under her gunny-bag seat and brought her posterior crashing gently down on it. She now sat at a slight angle.

Kanta held up the empty glass, her fingers commanding a little jig of it, showing that she was done. A sudden 'Aila!' from somewhere almost made her drop it. She turned to see Manda gaping at the emptied basket. 'You sold them all?' she asked. 'Sold them all,' Kanta repeated. 'You hadn't come yesterday, so they all wanted extra today. I wrapped the money in a newspaper.'

Manda sank to her haunches and rummaged through her basket. She seemed surprised at how neatly everything had been put away. She picked through the stash of notes and coins. She looked up at Kanta and said, 'Thank you.' Kanta shook her head lightly, said, 'Mention not,' and looked away at her flowers, half of them unsold, wilting slowly in the sun.

Manda looked up at her after counting the money and called out, 'Uh Kanta!' A faint flicker of guilt came on like a tubelight across Kanta's face.

Manda said, 'This … this is too much.'

Kanta heaved a sigh of relief and said, 'There was high demand today, so … I quoted more.'

Manda held out a fifty-rupee note for her. 'No, no … why?' Kanta withdrew. Manda pressed, 'Arre, why not? You looked after my shop for me … sold everything … we're partners now.'

Kanta recoiled even further, 'No, no, I can't.'

'It's for Lakshmi … here,' Manda insisted. Kanta took it but seemed unsure. She took out a small purse, her podgy fingers struggling with the tiny zipper. She stuffed the note in, paused for a long moment and said, 'Thank you.' Manda brushed off the thought, 'Mention not,' and grinned. She swung the empty basket, light as a pillow, onto her head and chirped, 'I'll see you then, bye.'

Kanta lightly touched the string of gajra in her hair, swung her shoulders forward and propped herself with one hand to get up when … 'Kanta?' It was Manda's voice.

Kanta froze mid-motion, then sank her bum back where it belonged, slowly and gently, so as not to squash her precious cache. Then she looked up at Manda, the colour from her face starting to drain.

Manda said, 'Can I have a gajra?'

The gajra swayed seductively in Manda's hair, as if mimicking her waist as she walked. She stopped next to a kulfi seller. A weather-beaten hand pierced a little stick into the open, wide end of a cold steel cone and turned the cone over. The hand gently massaged the cone, easing the kulfi out with the stick and held it up for Manda.

A band of fishermen dragged their whale-like boat out of the choppy waters onto the beach. Under the hungry afternoon sun, as they hauled in a large net bulging with fish, their dark muscles gleamed with sweat. From where she sat, some distance off on a low broken wall, Manda watched them intently. A thick drop dripped off the tip of the kulfi as she docked it in her mouth and then slid it out slowly, dragging its cold underside along her warm quivering tongue. Her basket, lying lazily on a rock beside her, gaped.

The sun had turned a flaming red by now. Hot and aching, it waited to sizzle into the cool of the sea.

Manda walked home. How surprising, she thought to herself, that the only day she hadn't sat by her fish, each and every one of them got sold. Just the thought alone made her feel warm all over.

When Manda reached the Versova Village bus stop she looked around and spotted a bunch of little boys standing in a group some way off. One little fellow shadow-practised a late cut with a cricket bat. Sachin stood in the centre. He tossed a coin up in the air. Watching the coin begin its descent, he spotted his mother, and came scurrying up to her. Behind him, the pack of boys converged on the clattering coin like squirrels.

Manda held a hot golden bhutta out to Sachin. Grinning, he ripped the leaves off it and took a big greedy chomp. As he chewed, pangs of salivation cracking like lightning through his jaws, Manda said, 'Do you want to spend the night at Amol's?'

Sachin nodded vigorously to the rhythm of his chewing.

An ochre glass bottle, bathed in a shaft of evening sunlight stood tall in the centre of a cane chataai. Manda's hand slid a long stalk of a red rose gently down its throat. Her hair hung about her shoulders, wet black ropes, undone.

A satin sheet billowed, stretching like a yawn, onto a low bed. Manda tucked the edges of the sheet in. It was wine purple with lighter mauve ripples streaming all across it. It seemed like a piece of the deepest part of the sea.

Manda held a tubelight around its slim waist and twisted it slightly, disconnecting the small conductors at the ends from their sockets. She then screwed a milky bulb into a socket on the far wall and pulled the curtains closed. At the flick of a switch, the bulb came on, its clouded yellow glow melting over the room like mango ice cream over a hot gulab jamun.

Manda tapped some gravy from a large ladle into the palm of her hand and blew on it till it cooled. Then she licked it and swirled it around her tongue. Her eyes lit up. She paddled the simmering gravy in the kadhaai with renewed enthusiasm, peering into it as if expecting a genie to emerge. The gajra had resumed its rightful place in her hair. From the corner of her eye she noticed her empty basket leaning tiredly against the wall, mouth open in a yawn.

In the slightly steamed-up mirror, the tip of Manda's little finger slid along the inside curve of her lower eyelid, leaving a thick black trail of kajal. She was disturbed by a slight movement behind her and turned to see Sachin running out of the room. Her heart missed a beat. She summoned him sternly, 'Sachin! Your homework?'

Blinking like a dormouse caught unawares by a flashlight, he held his school bag up innocently and mumbled, 'I'm doing it with Amol.' Manda recovered, turned back to the mirror and said nonchalantly, 'So run, you'll get late.' Sachin hovered for a bewildered moment and then was gone in a puff.

Manda stared into the bathroom mirror long and languorously

and brought the black-tipped finger up to her reflection. She touched it to the glass where her cheek was, left a thick black spot, smiled shyly and said, 'Kisi ki nazar na lag jaaye.'

And the sea swallowed up the sun.

Kanta's podgy hand struggled to scrape the scales off a large fish with a big blunt knife. Lakshmi stood in the doorway, watching with round, beady eyes.

A slim stream of steaming white water poured out as Manda strained the rice. There was a sound at the door. She shook the water out of the vessel and thumped it down just as a man's voice burst into the house, 'Arre, whose house is this now?'

Manda pushed a strand of hair from her wet forehead and smiled to herself as the voice continued, 'Manda, you did this?' Manda straightened the front of her saree and turning, said loudly, 'Milind, you won't believe what happened today ...' and looked in the direction of the empty fish basket. The basket laughed silently.

Milind burst in through the kitchen doorway and said, 'How'd you guess?' Manda looked at him perplexed.

'Here, Shashikant, take a look ...' And another man, slightly older, appeared in the doorway right behind Milind, beaming at Manda. Manda stared in mild shock.

'*This* is Manda,' Milind continued, 'God knows how she guessed you were coming!' Manda lowered her eyes, touched the gajra in her hair. 'Oye, why you being coy now?' he asked. Manda shifted uneasily. Milind continued regardless, 'He's my old friend Shashikant, remember, I told you about him? This is his second visit to Mumbai.' The two men exchanged a strange look and laughed. Manda just looked, the curve of her smile loosening fast.

'Remember,' he said, 'I told you about the time he came here for his college admission? Him and that college lift!' And the two men cracked up. Milind stepped closer to Manda as he spoke. 'This rascal … he stuck chewing gum on the fifth-floor and ground-floor buttons.'

Shashikant guffawed, 'Yeah, chewing gum … and the lift ran up and down by itself all day …'

'… like a Borivli fast,' completed Milind. And they both cracked up again. Milind suddenly noticed his wife didn't look too comfortable. He came closer and pushed his eyebrows up inquiringly. Shashikant caught the cue and disappeared from the doorway.

'Aye, did I do something wrong?' he asked. Manda just shook her head, 'No, it's just that I …' And Shashikant's voice cut in, 'Milind, where do I leave my bags?' Milind turned, 'Right there … by the door,' and left the kitchen.

Manda stared crestfallen at the kitchen door. Milind reappeared, saw the look on her face, came up to her and said, 'I should have asked you before bringing him here, no?'

'No, no, it's not that,' Manda protested weakly. Milind tried to comfort her, 'Don't worry, he'll be gone tomorrow. I'll just get him a drink and you can stuff him with finger-licking food so that he passes out in the living room itself, okay?' He winked naughtily. He turned to leave again when Manda reached for him and exploded, 'Isoldallthefish!'

In a flash, Milind turned, said 'Aila! Thanks for reminding me … this fellow …' and Shashikant reappeared at the kitchen door. 'He's threatened to drown himself in the sea if you don't make your special fish tonight.'

And as Milind laughed, Manda's eyes became hypnotized circles.

'From the minute he landed, he's been saying he's hungry, but I didn't let him eat anything for the last two hours so that he could save his appetite for the yummiest fish curry on the Konkan coast,' said Milind proudly.

Manda just stood, frozen, and smiled faintly.

Milind snapped his fingers, 'Come now, let's go get a khamba.' He turned to Manda, 'You need anything? For the curry or something?' Manda just shook her head numbly from side to side.

Kanta's podgy hands filled the cleaned-out entrails of the fish with a deep orange paste. The fish trembled in her firm hands as she forcefully stuffed it. Beside her, Lakshmi trembled with anticipation.

The main door slammed shut, sending a slight shudder through the house. Manda slowly crumpled to the floor and sat there scratching her head.

The large fish filled up the pan as it fried. A flat ladle squeezed itself underneath it and flipped it over. Happy Lakshmi sucked in some saliva, 'Ssssss . . .' while the gas flame threw small shadows of doubt all across Kanta's grim face.

Manda stared as the moon's dim glow spilt in from under the curtains and spread slowly across the floor. There was a flurry of small sharp knocks on the door. Her eyelids beat nervously to the rhythm of the knock.

She hadn't even opened the door fully when little Sachin

pushed through the parting and scampered past her legs. Manda lunged for his shoulders making him jump out of his skin. She explained the situation to him, her hands flailing about to the nervous sound of her jangling bangles. She pointed at the empty bewildered basket a couple of times and shook Sachin like a leaf until he nodded confusedly. She ended with, 'Now go look in the village, see if any fish is available, anywhere, at any price. Understood?' And she held out a hundred-rupee note folded twice down the middle. 'Hurry!'

Sachin nodded slowly, plucking the note from her fingers. He turned to leave when Manda stopped him again, 'If you find one, I'll buy you a cricket bat tomorrow.'

Sachin came alive like a headlight switched on, and dashed out of the door.

The fish lay bathed in bubbling gravy, as a dish eclipsed it. Kanta looked a little disturbed. Lakshmi sat with her head lowered nearby, weeping over chopped onions.

Manda stood before the bathroom mirror, a rag wrapped around her forefinger. She was rubbing the black kajal spot clean. She tried not to look at herself in the reflection.

Sachin turned away from yet another roadside shack. He trotted down the road, peeking around every corner. A stray dog, its tail wagging furiously, fell in step behind him. Suddenly Sachin froze. He sniffed the air. The dog stopped and sniffed the air too. An aroma was drifting out of a nearby window. In its verandah sat a young girl threading some flowers by the shaky light of a gas lamp. She didn't notice Sachin as he stepped up to the window and sniffed.

Fish.

Cooked.

He imagined the new cricket bat in his hands. He imagined swinging it. He imagined the sweet cracking sound it made against the deuce ball. He imagined the ball soaring for a six. And then he peeked around the corner. The smell was coming from behind the house.

The kitchen window was ajar. There was a pan on the choolha. The source of the aroma. Like a hungry kitten he looked around for a way to get in. The dog behind him barked once. Sachin turned to it and signalled it to shut up.

Manda ground her anxiety with an assortment of spices into a paste. Even if Sachin did get the fish she would still need a couple of hours to get it ready. Of all the days, why did this have to happen today? Idiot Milind. Stupid fisherman. Let me get my hands on a fish. First I'll slap him on the head with it. Idiot.

Just then, a shrill voice hacked the darkness, 'Arre, Sachin?'

Knees knocking, he turned to face mammoth Kanta. She flashed him the sweetest smile, 'What're you doing here?'

'N … nothing …' he stammered, turned and fled, chased by the dog. Kanta frowned thoughtfully, her forehead bunching up in dunes.

Manda began to sweat. The very work that seemed so delightful till about an hour ago now seemed thick with drudgery. There was a flurry of small sharp knocks on the door again.

The doors parted. Sachin's white face peered up at Manda from the dull lamplit darkness. His shirt was drenched with sweat.

Her eyes enquired silently. He pushed his lower lip out and shook his head. Deflated, she looked down at her feet. A high-pitched voice called out from the shadows, 'Aye Sachin, chal …'

Sachin held out the hundred-rupee note apologetically. He looked at his mother, concerned. Manda took it, closed her eyes and tilted her head saying, 'Go … don't worry.' Inside Sachin's head, the new cricket bat disappeared from his hands with a 'poof'. Manda opened her eyes just as Sachin turned …

… to reveal Lakshmi, framed by two crisp pigtails, holding a covered dish in her outstretched hands. Sachin froze. He watched Lakshmi hold the dish up towards Manda. Manda looked at her quizzically. Amol appeared and dragged a gaping Sachin away.

Manda lifted the lid. A large cooked fish stared up at her. She staggered slightly. Quickly, regaining her composure she replaced the lid. Lakshmi looked quite sullen, her lips curved downwards with the weight of her petulant cheeks. Manda asked slowly, 'Did … did your mother make this?' Lakshmi nodded, her stiff pigtails wagging up and down. 'Why? She's never sent me fish before?' thought Manda to herself. Then she grabbed the gift and said, 'Tell her I said thank you,' and patted Lakshmi on the top of her head.

Lakshmi looked like she was going to cry. She said, 'Sorry.' Manda asked why. Lakshmi curved the ends of her mouth further downwards and shrugged her shoulders. She didn't seem very much like talking, that too with the woman because of whom she was being deprived of the fish she had waited all day to sink her little milk teeth into. 'Ma said,' she mumbled.

Manda nodded disinterestedly, flashed a fake smile and turned to go inside, quickly shutting the door behind her.

She hurried over to the stove to put the dish on for a quick heat-up. There was a soft rap at the door again.

Outside, Lakshmi was still there, looking sulky. She said softly, as if trying to suppress the urge to bawl, 'She wants the plate back.'

'Tell her I'll bring it to the market tomorrow,' Manda replied and shut the door on her face.

Milind and Shashikant, sitting cross-legged on the kitchen floor, licked their fingers repeatedly after every mouthful. Manda heaped fish curry into Shashikant's plate while Milind shovelled some hungrily into his mouth. Floating out of his stupor, Milind asked, 'How come you've never made this curry before?'

Manda smiled coyly and touched the gajra in her hair. 'I just learnt it today,' she said, 'from the neighbour.'

In the corner, the basket seemed to have slipped onto its back, its mouth frozen open in a laugh.

Rs 4.50

On the other side of the ticket was a lucky draw coupon. I couldn't tell what the prize was. That bit had torn off when the bus conductor ripped the ticket from his stack.

When I told her about it, she said, 'What was ripped off was the price one pays for being lucky.'

CROSSES

The march of the crosses was arrested by a naught. Two crosses headed eastwards along the top row. Two headed south. Two headed diagonally. But they were thwarted each time by a naught. It was how Raju bided his time. Killing people was not the romantic job the world made it out to be. A big chunk of his life was obstructed by naughts.

If Aslam hadn't shown him how to pick these new dimple-keyed locks they put on doors these days, he'd be up on the terrace of this building right now, getting slow-roasted by the sun. That would have been a naught.

He had his rifle nestled in the window grill now. And his bottom nestled in a broken bucket. It was all he could find. And he needed the elevation. What a waste of space these flats were, he thought. The owners wouldn't sell them because they always wanted more than they were offered. And they wouldn't put them out on rent because they were afraid their tenant would 'squat'. And they wouldn't live in them either, letting mice, mosquitoes and pigeons take over instead. No wonder Allwyn takes these suparis. His house isn't even big enough for a double bed. We swapped homes for his wedding night, smirked Raju, and drew another nine-box grid with his pencil on the wall. He put a cross in the middle box, when some movement caught his eye. The tip of the pencil broke.

He watched the window through the cross hairs on his rifle telescope. In it, a plump middle-aged woman was looking down and shouting at someone. She held an empty dirty bucket in her hand. Clearly it must have been filled with garbage a few moments back. Most of which must be on someone's unsuspecting head now. Raju watched, adjusting the telescope till the woman was right in the centre of the little black cross. As the cross went blurry, she came into sharp focus. And he muttered to himself, 'bang'. It's her balding husband he seeked.

Raju's finger, taut with anticipation, started to gently massage the trigger, expending the tension. Through the viewfinder, the plump woman appeared tiny, her arms held out at right angles to her body, her legs held together, straight as Jesus'. As Raju watched, her head tilted slightly to her right and she hung there as if nailed to the cross inside his rifle-scope. Raju just watched, with one eye, till the woman's stigmata started to bleed, and then he took his eye off the scope. He looked once towards the window. She was gone.

Raju often saw his target crucified this way, like they'd been sacrificed for some mysterious betterment of man, like the Son of God was. But no one knew then what was to follow the act, argued Raju to himself. Every assassination thus felt like a personal mission, since there's nothing unholy about a crucifixion. It's preordained almost. A death whose time has come. And he's the unlucky sonofabitch that gets to 'bear the cross' of the cleansing. How ironic.

Although, he managed to make a healthy living while he was

at it. The ones that knew him feared the silent power he wielded. And the ones he killed, he derived his position of strength from the fact that he knew them, could see them, but they couldn't, him. All that talk of it being much easier from a distance, with a gun, than up close, getting your hands dirty, was just that – talk. He'd told Aslam once, take your fingers off those keys and wires and put them on a trigger for once. It's not an easy thing to press. 'I can't hear them breathe when I kill them, but I sure as hell can see the look in their eyes.'

Sometimes that 'look in their eyes' was one of abject fear. For sometimes he was spotted before he pulled the trigger. It didn't matter to the job at hand. Because the shock made his target immobile for a long moment, enough time to hammer a bullet into their head. But it did compel him to see in their eyes not just the usual realization of dying, spreading like a film across their iris, but the apprehension of oncoming death, and the flicker of having recognized him as the bearer of the same. At such times, even if he was a kilometre from his target, the distance smashed into nothing, and he could taste their cold sweat on his tongue. It stirred his heartbeat just a little. And his head gently swam. It was strange. It was the taste of vomit at the mouth of his throat. But it was heady.

In a strange way, it gave Raju comfort, his sense of power in flicking that switch. It was bereft of morality. He didn't sit on judgement on those he killed. Which is why he never entered the conversations that Allwyn and Hilaal had. They were always bitter. Always seeking redemption in the crimes they committed. Raju was aware he operated outside of the moral framework of the world he inhabited. So he kept himself from ever having to have an opinion on it.

Yes, he didn't sleep well at night. And his targets and their wives and children often crucified themselves of their own accord inside his scope. But he had a gun. And like it or not, they'd all live and die at his behest. It was worth it just for that. He caught some movement at the window again, and snapped back into position.

It was the wife again. She was waving her arms like a monster and screaming at someone. Raju swung his rifle to the left and spotted a monkey on the adjoining terrace. It snarled at the wife and threw something at her. Raju swung his rifle back at the window to see it slam shut. He muttered a curse, swung back to the monkey, his finger tightening on the trigger. The monkey stayed still at the edge of that terrace for a long while. Raju waited, wondering if he should just get it over with, get the monkey out of the way so that the window opens again. Or should he not interfere? No good ever came of drifting from the original plan. He waited, hoping the monkey would appear crucified on his cross hairs. He'll take that as a sign and pop the little fucker's skull open.

But the monkey was no Christ.

And just as Raju took in a quick breath to pull the trigger, the monkey looked right at him. Raju froze. In the viewfinder the monkey wasn't half a kilometre but barely a foot away. The monkey snarled at him. Raju nearly shot it when it jumped out of sight. Raju swung the rifle to the left and caught it in the cross hairs once more. But the monkey jumped again. Raju found it and strained at the trigger. The monkey paused, then leaped out of frame. The monkey jumped about the terrace like a crazy ball let loose. Raju followed it with the tenacity and adroitness of a video gamer. Every once in a while it'd stop, look right at Raju, and before Raju could get his wits about him, the monkey would spring again. For the first time in his sharpshooting career, Raju's brow broke into a single bead of cold sweat. The drop trickled around his brow and slid down the side of his open eye.

He took his eye off the telescope and wiped his brow with his sleeve. When he looked again, the monkey had disappeared. Raju swung the rifle this way ... and that ... up ... down ... no sign of the monkey. He took a deep breath to slow down his pulse and was readjusting the focus on the scope when the monkey popped into the lens, and snarled! Raju tumbled back in shock, his behind smashing through his broken-bucket seat. He quickly jabbed his finger back onto the trigger, ready to pull.

The monkey was right outside the window grill now. It grabbed the mouth of the rifle barrel with both hands and peered in. Raju watched it, silent. The monkey's attention was riveted to the gun. It had tired of Raju a while back. It bit the nozzle tip, sucked on it, as if expecting a sweet nectar to come squirting out of its depths. It stayed there for a few long moments, a third of the rifle barrel inside its mouth, blinking confusedly. Raju realized his finger was still tensed on the trigger, and he relaxed it, and slowly slid it out.

Raju pushed himself away from the window and watched the monkey. It was strange how fearless it was. Blissfully unaware that the thing in his mouth could blow the contents of it's head right out a gaping hole in the back, in one split second. It didn't fear the gun. And hence it didn't fear him. Which took Raju's mind to the window he had been watching all afternoon. The bald man in the window would fear him, because he would fear his gun. Because he'd know what a gun can do.

Raju looked at the monkey bite down on the gleaming black

metal pipe like it would a branch, expecting it to submit to the clench of its teeth. In that long minute Raju realized that the gun was not his weapon of death. He was the gun's. The gun was the carrier, the executioner. The gun crucified. The gun barked orders at Raju to pull the trigger. And the gun barked bullets. The gun was a dog. The gun was God. No one feared him. Stripped of the gun, Raju would be as annoying as the plump woman in the window, as morally invalid as Allwyn, as impotent as Aslam, a criminal, whose brains could be blown out as easily with another rifle. Even this one. Because he knew what it could do. Not like this monkey. That didn't.

By now the monkey had grown bored of the flavourless gun, and hung by one arm from the window grill, gently swinging about in the late afternoon breeze, staring into empty space. Raju watched it, immobile. The monkey suddenly let go of the grill, dropped down on the parapet, jumped across to the neighbouring window, clambered up a pipe, hopped over to the next terrace, bounded across it and disappeared into a tree.

Raju slumped down on the ground, and stared at his gun. The far window opened again. And a balding man leaned out and lit himself a cigarette.

On the wall, in the 'crosses and naughts' grid, a cross sat alone in the centre box.

1984

The boat was pulled by the current and it disappeared into the manhole. The metal lid had been propped open by a bamboo stick.

Pappu swam in the middle of the road.

Mom sliced boiled potatoes and sprinkled salt, pepper and sev on the pieces.

Dad tore a sheet of newspaper into four and folded me another boat. The headlines read *28 die in Hooghly ferry capsize* and *Indira Gandhi to visit today*.

BOTTLES

Red.

Yellow.

Orange.

Green.

Pink.

White.

Purple.

I picked blue.

Surrounded by tall glass bottles filled with the coloured syrups, Salim, his lips dark red with paan juice, his eyes jet black with soorma, his hair a shocking mehndi orange, held a big block of ice with a green checkered muslin cloth, and grated it along a slicing blade embedded in a small wooden plinth. His other hand was cupped below the blade, to collect the nearly powdered ice as it fell. Handful by careful handful, the crushed ice was slipped into the four glasses standing empty before him. The ice block was gently but quickly returned to its jute sack bed in the corner of the table cart, the sack folded over it so that it wouldn't melt too fast in the mid-April summer heat of Calcutta.

Salim slid a small hatch open in the tabletop, his hand

plunged in, and two big yellow lemons emerged from the chamber inside the cart. He thumped them gently on the wood plinth, rolled them around with the full palm of his hand till they turned a little yellower, and with one skilful swipe of the knife he sliced them both in two. He popped one hemisphere into a pronged lemon squeezer, held it over one glass and pressed it close. Lemon juice squirted like rain over the ice. When the squeezer opened up, the dry corpse of the lemon wedge was quickly chucked onto the lemon graveyard by the side of the cart and Salim proceeded to squeeze the life out of the next one.

The secret hatch slid open again. I tried to peek in but Salim slammed it shut and grinned his wet red grin at me, his kohl-lined eyes twinkling mischievously. A bottle of ice-cold water had emerged. Standing around the cart in sweaty white shirts stuck to our skins and our maroon ties loosened around our little necks, we must have all remembered our mothers telling us how many germs there might be in that water that Salim fills in his bottles from the municipal tankers. But we quickly chased those thoughts away. We loved watching Salim work his hypnosis on us. Glass by glass, the ice was splashed with a little chilled water.

And then Salim reached for the coloured bottles.

Our tongues went wet with little bursts of saliva.

And our throats went dry with anticipation.

The bottles formed a miniature fortress wall along the three edges of the rectangular cart. Each glass bottle had a small hole pierced into its metal cap. And when Salim held the bottle some distance above the glass and tilted it with a dramatic flourish, the syrup would shoot out in a delicious projectile and swirl the contents of the glass with colour. It was yellow for little Qamber. His eyes went round when the yellow syrup squirted out of the bottle and plunged into the glass. Then the bottle went back into its wooden groove along the periphery of the thela, and Salim glanced at Vijit with the knowing look of a magician about to entrap his audience with the next act, as he reached for green.

Vijit gaped as green syrup brought his glass alive. Unable to contain himself Vijit reached his finger out to get a taste of his drink. Salim, feigning annoyance, stopped, stepped away from the cart and just looked at Vijit. It was his way of saying that the show was over. The rest of us, shocked, stared at Vijit. The senior boy from class six knocked Vijit on the head. Scared, he mumbled, 'Sorry.' Salim lifted his finger at Vijit as if warning him this was the last time. Vijit took one step back. Salim took one step forward, and slowly reached for blue. The cool sky blue. My blue. He did this very slowly, as if punishing us all for our impatience.

When the small blue fountain splashed into my glass a bubble burst gently inside my head.

The senior boy's drink was purple. Kala khatta. I never understood why the bigger boys liked a little sour to corrupt their sweet.

Salim then slipped a large pepper-shaker out of one of the bottle grooves, spun it around in his hand and shook masala into each glass. He reached for an empty glass, turned it upside down, held it over the open mouth of each glass by turn and shook the contents vigorously. Ready, they were handed out – purple, yellow, green and blue.

With the first sip, a breeze picked up across the Park Circus Maidan, snaked in through the space between my shirt buttons and caressed my burning skin. The second sip travelled to my finger and toe tips making them shiver slightly in glee. Three more boys appeared around the cart. We continued to sip our drinks, our eyes riveted on Salim's hands as he went through the same hypnotic procedure for the next four glasses. I suddenly realized I didn't have one rupee to pay him today. It was 3.30 p.m. and I needed the three rupees I had for the hand-rickshaw ride home. 'Salim chacha,' I said, trying to phrase the rest of the sentence in my head, when Salim figured it out, flashed me the dark red insides of his mouth and tilted his head to one side, indicating that I could pay him later. I had lost count of the number of one rupees I owed him. I suspect now that he had too.

When a parent was late picking up his little son, he wouldn't bother checking with the watchman or the principal. He'd come straight to Salim. Because most times a scared little boy would find comfort at Salim's cart, sucking happily on a crushed-ice lolly, watching mesmerized as Salim worked his icy magic for scores of other kids. Salim knew each of the hundreds of kids by name. He knew most of their parents too, even if their parents didn't know him. If the child in question wasn't around his thela, Salim would know where he might be now, playing in the table-tennis room or running around in the field inside. How he knew that, no one knew. But he knew. And it was strange, because Salim had never once, in all those years, been inside the school premises. He appeared outside the main gate around noon. And disappeared from there just before the sun did.

He was there every day of school. And every holiday too, ready to serve some 'thanda' to any kid that might have come by to play a hot game of cricket in the school field. He was there, chewing paan, grinning, looking cool in the shade of the mango tree under which he stood. Salim never perspired. And Salim never ever drank any nimbu-paani. I remember asking him once if he'd ever tasted his own baraf golas. Flashing his red juicy grin, he had said, 'Bahut thanda hai!'

Salim didn't sell nimbu-paani and baraf-golas for a living. He sold them because it gave him a reason to live. He was the only constant outside the gates of Don Bosco School for years. The little kids grew up. The grown-up kids left for college. The teachers changed. The gate watchman changed. The principal changed too. The colour of the school's walls went from yellow to white and back to yellow again. Coca Cola replaced Kwality ice cream. Plastic bottles replaced glass. But Salim remained. As steadfast as the khamba of a sundial, the shadows changing manically around him. The low boundary walls of the school compound were raised. Salim could no longer peek inside over them, to know where his little patrons might be. Parents stopped coming to him to find out where their kids were. Over time, the children stopped coming to him too. The thought of germs in his water had started to take a stronger hold on the children's imaginations. Bottled Pepsi seemed a much safer option.

But Salim stayed there, under the mango tree, squirting coloured syrups into glasses filled with crushed ice, shaking them vigorously for the peons of the school when they were done with their duties. Salim stayed there, watching little children grow up and leave, and in some cases watching them return with their own children. Salim stayed there till even the mango tree disappeared, gobbled up by a widened road. Salim was pushed further away from the main gate, to the corner of the pavement, where hand-rickshaw drivers came to him for his nimbu-paani. To the rickshaw-wallahs, his coloured syrups held no thrall. To keep his expenses low, he started sticking to the basics.

Ice.

Water.

Lemon.

Sugar syrup.

The coloured bottles disappeared. His hair turned white. He didn't feel the urge to line his eyes with soorma any more. And the paan habit had given him oral cancer. He raised hell if someone didn't have three rupees for the glass just consumed.

Salim now did this for a living.

Once in a while on a hot afternoon you might spot him sitting on a brick by his cart, his torn kurta drenched with sweat, watching the little boys pour out of the school gates into their waiting air-conditioned cars. If you look closely, you'll see him holding a glass of his own nimbu-paani. He looks at it curiously before he takes his first sip.

BEING IN THE MIDDLE

Mejho looks like he's fifty-five. But he's really just a ripe old forty-two. He was born in the middle, with a brother each born before and after him. And so he started life on the fence.

While his younger brother was sent to school and ended up in a salaried job somewhere in Siliguri, his elder had joined their father in the fields, and so naturally staked claim to all the farming when their father died. Mejho, uneducated, unskilled and landless, came to Calcutta, where he earned his first rupee at the age of ten carrying someone's bag off a train into a waiting taxi. Soon he gave up coolie-ing and started selling moori, carrying a large sack of puffed rice through the streets of Calcutta, shouting 'moori … moori' and watching for windows to open and housewives to beckon him up musty building stairs so that he could weigh out the moori for them on his hand-held weighing scales. All through, he had been a man who had little to say. The only words that escaped his mouth were 'moori' and the price of it.

He never argued, complained, opined or expressed emotion.

Until he got married.

Neelima was his father's best friend's middle daughter,

sandwiched unlike him, not just between two sisters, one elder and one younger, but also six brothers. Mejho liked Neelima the instant he set eyes on her. On their marriage night, he sneaked in a paper thonga under his dhoti, because he had seen that she hadn't eaten a single morsel all day. And they spent all night munching on moori and laughing about being in the middle. Actually it was Neelima who spoke. Mejho just listened. And listening with all his heart, he fell in love.

Back in Calcutta, he'd finish his rounds as quickly as his strong legs would carry him around the streets, so that he could rush back to his Neelima. Before marriage, he had begun to think of other trades he could try. There was going to be an extra mouth to feed, and that would need extra income. But now, he had dropped all thoughts of plying another business in the evenings because that would mean another four to five hours spent away from Neelima. Not just that, he now rushed through the streets so fast with the moori that he failed to notice half the housewives that called out to him. The moori that came home with him every night, he and Neelima ate as jhaal moori – with mashed boiled potatoes, salt and green chillies.

He discovered that Neelima hated cooking. But it didn't matter as long as there was enough moori.

As time passed, Mejho's income dwindled. They started to eat moori in the mornings too, Neelima chattering like an excitable bird and Mejho listening quietly, all the creases in his brow ironed out by the sound of her voice. Soon, Neelima contracted pneumonia and died.

The doctor, suspecting malnutrition, asked Mejho about their diet. 'Moori,' said Mejho innocently, the word conjuring up a life that already seemed like it had been left way behind in the remote past.

Mejho's aunts, uncles and his elder brother got him married again, this time to Neelima's younger sister. As was the norm, most families in the village tried to pack their daughters off to the city, a golden chance for them to wrap up all parental duties. Being in the middle, Mejho didn't have much say in the matter, though the last thing he wanted was for Neelima to be replaced this fast. And if anything, Neelima's death had taught him that two mouths to feed needs double the income, and hence double the effort. And that love and income in his world cannot coexist.

The sack of moori disappeared from Mejho's head, replaced by large heavy baskets that he couldn't take off his head without a helping hand from a passer-by. He took to selling vegetables by day and pots by evening. He also started to wear his voice out by screaming non-stop all day. There were words inside him, words he'd never be able to say to Neelima ever again.

So he twisted those words around and screamed out exhortations in song, '*Aayiyo babu vaayiyo babu baingan leke jaayiyo re, aayiyo babu vaayiyo babu baingan leke jaayiyo*'; in rhyme, '*Matka bolo, maatir matka, taaja toyri, ekdom taatka*'; in story, '*Jeerey-aaloo baanaben, khokha-khukhi ke khaawaaben, na khele motor-aaloo, shetaa-o niye eshechhi*'.

He haggled endlessly with customers, deaf to the sound of his own voice sometimes, but talking nonetheless, hoping he'll run out of things to say. Things he only wanted to say to Neelima, but now couldn't.

When he would get home late at night, his wife would be

waiting, hungry and expectant. He'd give her the vegetables he had saved for her, without a word. And as she'd rush in to cook it for him, he'd sit on the step outside their shanty, open up a small paper thonga, slowly munch on moori and fall asleep right there.

His young wife would emerge from the room and could never muster up the courage to wake him for supper. To her, he was a man who never spoke and clearly didn't appreciate being spoken to. The first few weeks of their marriage, she fell asleep hungry, hoping he'd wake up suddenly in the middle of the night and demand to be fed. But he never did. By the time she awoke at dawn, Mejho would be long gone. Soon, she got used to it, and cooked for herself, ate, and fell asleep. Mejho never found out what an exceptional cook Neelima's younger sister was.

Mejho also never found out her name.

Soon, she left him. He never cared to find out where she'd gone. The only thing he cared about was his moori and mashed boiled potato with salt and green chillies, which he ate thoughtfully each night and each morning, hoping that he too would contract what the doctor said Neelima had.

Mejho was tired of being in the middle.

REFUGEE

She was sitting on the single step outside her shanty.

I picked a water balloon out of the tub, held it gently to my ear and shook it to hear the water gurgle inside. I threw it over the railing and ducked out of sight. I heard it land with a wet splotch. And grinned when I heard her frail old voice scream some expletives in a Bengali dialect I didn't understand.

THE APOLOGY

Dying, Abbu tells me why.

'During the war, your Ammi was a POW. Nine months later you were born.

'I'm sorry I could never bring myself to look at you,' he says, as he looks away, 'because you don't look like me.'

BINDI

A Sinhalese bullet targetted Amma's bindi. So, for years, I hid mine.

Tonight, my boat hits Indian shores.

By dawn, a small red sun will rise on my clouded forehead.

A RIVER OF COTTON

On the densely forested island of Bali in the Sunderbans, thirty-four-year-old Moyna, who became a grandmother last month, looks at her white saree, its pale whiteness rippling like the surface of the river on which her husband sets himself afloat. He used to be a farmer, before the gradually encroaching sea submerged his arable land and filled it with so much salinity that he couldn't grow anything on it any more. He took to venturing into the mangrove creeks, much to the displeasure of the other fishermen, to look for fish and crabs, along with the stray beehive. In all these years, there had rarely been a night when Moyna hadn't felt her husband's body next to hers when she went to sleep. That guarantee had now run out.

The wives of hunters and fishermen in the Sunderbans wrap themselves in white sarees the minute their husbands set forth on their forest forages. A white saree is a widow's cocoon. They have a heightened sense of the uncertainty that preys on their daily lives. A heightened sense that never degenerates into self-pity, never gets magnified to calamitous proportions. It just is. A manifestation perhaps of their ingrained awe for the power that nature wields; her whims, her fury and her unconditional bounty.

These wives submit to the looming possibility of widowhood when they bid their husbands goodbye at the river's edge.

When the husbands return, if they do, the sarees are duly—and with much relief—exchanged for coloured ones. And those whose husbands do not return, or return incomplete—some part of them having been torn off by a tiger—remain silently ensconced in the cold confines of their white saree without so much as a wail. It isn't fortitude as much as it is an acceptance of their place in the scheme of the world they were born into.

Today, Moyna enters their fold, as she slowly wraps herself in white, aware that her husband might return like Niyoti's brother did, without both arms and one leg, the stumps of all three chewed through to the bone by an alarmed tiger. Or what might return would just be a story, told by other fishermen, of how they found his boat standing in one remote corner of the creek, and there was no sign of Torua, except for a trail of footprints in the sludge that ended at a tree. Or he might return, his arms laden with fish and a honeycomb. And she will quickly tear the white saree off herself and set about grinding the moshla for a hearty meal of fish curry and rice. And they will have food to eat.

At least for a week. Before the white six-yard-long cotton river reclaims her. And another, many miles long, murmuring with the promise of some more food, beckons her husband into its folds.

MINE

He was mine. Until a company cleared our village, dug a mine.
He now wears khaki. I wear green.
We sow bullets in our land, to reap an iron harvest.

AMBUSH

The dam waters are deep. The troop is tense.

As they cross over into Naxal territory, one of the CRPF jawans asks their adivasi boatman, 'So where's your village?'

'Right below us,' he murmurs.

BUTTERFLIES ON STRINGS

Prologue

Sarkaar

It's a nearly full moon night. The rude glow from my mobile phone suddenly explodes in the darkness of our Tata Sumo car. It's one of those text messages that arrives in instalments. So I read it in bits, pretty certain many others too would be receiving the same text round about now.

'Peace from white …'

My gaze drifts from this small, harsh square of light to the window I'm sitting at. Outside, the landscape keeps changing shape. Under a charcoal-black sky, the light of the moon makes a large mango tree cast a shadow like a conjoined twin.

'Love from pink …'

Many valleys, between many hills that would generally be grey, would generally be mourning the loss of another day to the night, sink into an eerily green shroud tonight, a shroud being woven by the loose threads of light which drop out of the full moon, so full that she can hardly contain them.

For a moment I wonder where I got my poetic inclinations from. Couldn't be Dad. If there's anything I got from him, it's this job, surveying valleys for what lies beneath them.

'Development from green …'

Out of nowhere, a train slinks out of the dark like a panicked snake and peppers the landscape with a neat succession of brightly lit floating squares, slipping through the mountains' folds, in a straight line, as if stitching the fragmented night together.

'Power from red …'

It's a breathtaking sight. The valley seems right now like a little black cup of heaven, filling up to its brim with molten silver. Just then, we turn the corner and they reveal themselves.

Large, metal-jawed excavating machines, waiting at the bowl's edge with their mouths open. I should know. We put them there. This valley is now a factory floor.

The railway tracks pincer it – surgical scissors sliding into its bowels. The machines wait, their large sharp teeth poised to dig up the earth, rip out the mango tree, chew, soften and spit up its entrails, and straight-jacket it in concrete.

Once those roads are ready, it's the turn of the hills.

Large drills will descend roaring into the earth's molars and dig out bloodied cavities where there are none. Bauxite, they call it . . . the silver hidden deep inside those teeth. Gold to most who profit from it. Helps deliver iron to the rest of us. It almost sounds logical, the crudeness of it all.

As the valleys spin into the distance, I look back up at the moon. When we're done with every such valley in every such corner of the world, I tell her, we'll be coming for you. Suddenly she looks jaundiced.

'Knowledge from yellow.'

And we drive right out of the landscape. The rest of the message reads:

'. . . This holi will add all the colours to your life.'

Just then, Kothari's cellphone beeps. His soft snoring jams. He stirs, gropes his shirt pocket, excavates the silver phone, brings it up to his face and blinks sleepily into its ghostly blue glow. 'Holi,' he sneers, 'bhenchod!' And he turns to me and flashes his paan-brown teeth, hoping I'll ask what happened. I have no interest in the inner machinations of my idiot boss's mind. I grind my teeth, turn to him and ask, 'What happened, sir?'

'*They're* wishing us Happy Holi,' he spits. As if I didn't know that already, I want to say. 'Really?' I exclaim. 'Stuck in this kachra jungle when we should be in Gurgaon right now, making bhaang,' he scowls, '*We* survey the land, *we* find the bauxite, *we* bust our backs in these bullock-cart Sumos, while *they* smear themselves in gulaal and knock back the bhaang till they piss in their socks. Not fair saala.'

'Not fair,' I mutter. It pacifies him. But this mutter, I meant it. It's not fair.

It's not fair that I had to give up on a life teaching literature to work for a steel company.

It's not fair that hills this beautiful should have within their wombs things we need to kill them to get at.

It's not fair that every time I ask Kothari why the adivasi has to be shunted off his own land, so we can ruin it at leisure, he mumbles, 'demand-supply Sarkaar, demand-supply' and considers it enough said.

It's not fair that when I sit down to think about the larger picture, all of this actually makes sense to me.

It's not fair that this robs me of my sleep at night. Whereas Kothari can sleep as soundly as a corpse even in a car that rattles like a loose window in a storm. Why does he not feel any guilt?

Asshole.

Why?

Shifting uncomfortably in his seat now, Kothari stifles a burp, leans into the back of the driver's head and asks, 'Where exactly are we now?' The driver talks to the rear-view mirror. 'Lohhovalsa,' he says and his face shutters itself. 'Bhenchod, what kind of a name is that?' grumbles Kothari, fidgeting in his seat to get into a sleeping position again. Realizing the effort is futile, he turns to me and asks, 'Should we stop here tonight? It's on the survey map.'

1. Lohhovalsa

The village shimmered high up on the hill, as if being licked to sleep by some unseen tongue of fire. The unit was scared. And tired. Sushil didn't know which of the two he felt more. He stopped his racing mind for a moment, to think. He decided it would have to be 'tired'. The fifteen of them had already walked twelve kilometres through the jungles. The mere sight of this hill, looming before him like a large angry snake, made his knees wobble. But they couldn't stop, not now. He slipped his automatic rifle off his left shoulder and swung it onto his right.

This was the least they could do to stay alive. Walk. Almost every other convoy of CRPF jawans that had dared to move around on wheels in these parts had never made it back to their camp alive from their 'combing' operations. Sushil remembered helping clear the Malkangiri road of uniformed bodies last week. Once they had finished, they had spent another day looking for the heads that had belonged to those bodies.

It's what tribes used to do when they went to war.

But this can't be a 'war', thought Sushil, perturbed. The Maoists aren't a 'tribe' though some of them might be tribals. The CRPF certainly isn't. Which tribe hunts for a monthly salary?

Sushil's left shoulder throbbed with a raw pain. He touched it under his green camouflage shirt. It was bleeding. He clenched his jaw, spoke to his shoulder, and kept walking. Since, in the middle of an operation, there was never time to tend to a wound, he had learnt to speak to those parts of himself that would give up on him. He now told his left shoulder to stop bleeding. Please. And that if they made it back to camp alive tonight, he'd take care of it before dawn. Promise.

That reminded Sushil of the snake bite on his right ankle. Suddenly his ankle started to throb too. So he spoke to both of them – his ankle and his shoulder.

The primary health-care worker who had visited their camp

yesterday had wondered aloud as she sucked the venom out of his ankle and dressed the wound in haldi. She had said that the snakes here had bitten more CRPF soldiers in the last month than they had tribals in the last eighteen years she had been practising in that region. 'Why do you think?' Sushil had asked. She had looked up at him then with glassy eyes and said, 'The adivasi doesn't threaten the snake.'

The five of them took a deep breath and thundered into the village from its uphill entrance, making sure they announced their entry with a solitary gunshot, followed by as many shouts, broken pots, frightened livestock and kicked-in bamboo doors as possible. If any of the villagers tried to sneak out now, they'd be waylaid by the other two parties, cutting off the entrance to the forest on the right and the way uphill on the other side of the village. They knew this village like they knew their own morning stubble. And to think none of them had ever been this far inside the jungle before tonight. But then there's a lot you can learn from a widowed PHC worker threatened to being branded a 'Maoist sympathizer' unless she proved herself otherwise.

And being labelled a Maoist sympathizer in these parts robbed you of the right to resist a gang rape.

Sushil had never found this operation agreeable. Green Hunt, they called it. And rightly so, since most captured rebels were carried out of the jungle hung like 'game', their wrists and feet tied to bamboo sticks. Sushil wondered what stopped the government from roasting these people they captured, and eating them. 'If we're going to go so far,' he thought, 'we might as well go all the way.'

But he didn't raise his voice, not once. He needed the money he earned. Dissent would only earn him a court martial. And back home, there was no longer any land left that he could farm. So on nights such as this one, Sushil also spoke to his heart, telling it to stop bleeding, for now. That he'd tend to it in the morning. But when morning came he tried his best to ignore the deep, hollow pain that echoed through it.

It wasn't hard actually. There was always some other part of his body that required more immediate attention.

As the fifteen of them converged at the centre of the adivasi village, their rifles pointed, their eyes more fearful than furious, they saw the villagers gathered around a large bonfire. They had all gone statue-still, in the middle of some ritual. They seemed to Sushil like a tableaux frozen in time. Like he had just walked into a tribal museum, and was gaping at the central exhibit. But the breath heaving in those chests displaced that thought. All the adivasi men had bows slung across their chests, and a leather quiver of arrows on their backs. The little bits of metal pierced all over the women's faces flickered in the firelight. In another place, at another time, Sushil would've sworn they looked ethereal. But here, tonight, the sight of their raw, almost animal-like beauty made his bladder quiver. To keep himself from draining into his pants he cocked his rifle.

The sound broke the deadlock. Ranjan, the only jawan who spoke Oriya in the unit, asked the villagers where Singanna was. Thirty pairs of unflinching eyes stared back at him. Ranjan, his eyes darting about, inspecting the darkness beyond the perimeter of the fire's light, repeated the query, emphasizing 'Singanna', knowing, as did the rest of them, that there was very little chance the villagers understood Oriya, or any of the Indian republic's other languages, given that there were hundreds of tribal dialects in Orissa alone. But that name – Singanna – was sure to get a reaction.

And it did.

A young man, Ghenua, standing closest to the fire, breathing hard, as if he had been running fast, and had suddenly stopped just now, shook his head, glaring at Ranjan even as he did.

They had been told Singanna hailed from this village, Lohhovalsa, and that he had recently – after spending years fighting for tribal rights – turned rogue and joined the Maoists. What choice had he, wondered Sushil, when they had been briefed that evening. Things had now come to such a head that anyone who came close to questioning any of the state's decisions was now branded a 'sympathizer' and hunted down. But on the other hand, thought Sushil, perhaps it's the way I feel, maybe there's more to this than I'll ever know or understand. And that thought always brought him some peace. Because not knowing meant that you had to follow orders without question and so you wouldn't hesitate in combat. Which in turn meant you stood very little chance of being killed. Also, you continued to retain a job that paid. Even if not on time. Now, how many youngsters from his village in Chhattisgarh could claim *that*.

The pop and crackle of the bonfire was beginning to fill up this silent void. The sound also made them nervous. Ranjan now looked around, confused, not knowing what to do next. His eyes met Pradip's, who told him, in Hindi, to ask that young man if he knows Singanna. Ranjan muttered, 'Boss, they don't speak Oriya, and I don't speak their language.' Pradip, his shoulders starting to twitch, turned to Ghenua himself and barked in Hindi, 'We know Singanna is from this village. Now tell us where he is or we won't leave.'

Silence.

'Singanna, Singanna!' He repeated as he stomped his boots, hoping the action would scare somebody … anybody.

Sushil didn't much care for Pradip. Actually there was very little in Orissa Sushil cared much for.

Just then, Pradip saw Ghenua's hand reach for his bow. As Sushil yelled 'Pradip, no!' Pradip lunged for Ghenua and rammed his rifle butt into his chin. Ghenua fell. A dozen other hands reached for their bows. More boots stomped. Rifles got cocked. Gunshots fired into the sky. Women screamed. Before he knew it, Sushil was threatening some of the villagers with gunshots screaming 'Singanna? Singanna?' as if the chanting of that one word would absolve him of any wrong he was about to commit.

The bonfire was a lump of smoking ash when they dragged their hurting, tired selves down the hill, their arms laden with small sacks of foodgrain, and captive, dizzy chickens slung over their shoulders. They darted through the jungle in deathly silence. No one was quite sure of what they had just done. Thirteen breaths caught in a panicked choke once when Sushil stepped on a dry twig.

Only Pradip was calm.

While Kabir was numb with shock.

2. Kabir

'28 November 2008,' she says on the news. 'Two days.' 'Forty-eight hours.' With such emphasis like she was in some apocalypse movie trailer. They're still firing. From the hotel's windows. The gunshots are barking inside my head, bursting into red clouds. I snort another line. My sixth today. I ought to stop. I stare at the smoke on the TV screen. There are words all over it. Big bold letters. '26/11.' 'Mumbai under siege.' 'Terror.'

Terror. Noun.

Terrific. Adjective.

This powder's terrific. A phone rings. I mimic it, hoping it'll get irritated and stop. It stops. Knocking. On my room door. Ma's voice. Fuck. I didn't think she'd be up this late. I feel the buzz deserting me as the blood rushes back into my head.

'Kabir?'

'Haan?' I mumble, hoping she'll go away.

'Mallika called,' she says, waiting for a response from me. I'm fumbling to clear the little coke mound off my exam board. I'll need to turn on the exhaust fan in the loo, so that the room can lose the smell. What if she walks in now … but she never does that … but what if she does?

'Rahul is still inside the Taj,' she says.

And my hands start to tremble.

Standing outside the Taj hotel, turning away from the smoke still bleeding from its steeples, I look down at the vein in my right arm. It lies motionless under my skin like a mottled snake, black blotches everywhere I have pierced it with my needle. I open and close my fist a few times, feel the blood throb through the snake and fight back a sudden tear.

I start walking. Past the tired NSG commandos taking naps in the bus windows. Past blood-stained stretchers. Past cameras, agitated men and women with mikes, pads, pens, vada pavs, cigarettes, all looking at one another and at me like they're afraid it might be their turn to die next. I keep tripping over my own feet all the way to J.J. Hospital. But the rhythm of the walking calms my pounding heart. My vision is blurry. I picture my eyes bloodshot. Blood. Shot. Perfect words for a day like this one. Blood. Shot. Blood. At the hospital, I find a volunteer, get him to put my name down as a donor, trip in at the end of a very long queue of talkative people, and I freeze.

My blood still has last night's shit. Hell, I haven't given the cocaine a break all week. Ever since Rahul gave me that spiel about 'washing' up. Fuck, man. Fuck. I would've washed up you fucker. I would've washed the fuck up. Selfish prick, I am. Fuck. Would my blood really help save a life now? Or end one? What if they carry out tests before taking my blood? Shit. What if they send the reports home?

I step out of the queue and walk out of the hospital.

I stop on the opposite footpath and survey the mob inside. The men and women in those queues look desperate. What must their blood be like? Angry blood. Sad blood. Confused blood. Blood on the boil. Bad blood. Scarlet blood. Pink blood. Blue blood.

Blood that's never left a body.

Blood that's been shed before.

A blood. B blood. AB blood. O blood. Reluctant blood. Willing blood.

Hey, wait a minute, I'm not the only selfish one here. Hardly anyone got injured in the attacks. They got killed.

Rahul's dead.

He doesn't need blood.

He doesn't need anything.

My fingers start shaking again. I fish out a rolled joint, my last. I light it, suck on it hard and long, till I feel the floor of my lungs on fire. I open my mouth to scream. But a stream of white smoke escapes it. I think I'm about to fall. My arms flail, grab a lamp post. I crumple against it. I call it 'Mallika'. The lamp post hugs me back. I start to cry.

The buzz hits me like a needle jab to my brain. Do the dead need my tears? Am I crying for Rahul? Or am I crying for myself?

Ma doesn't leave till evening. Only when she's been gone ten minutes am I able to summon the courage to enter the house. I drink two bottles of water. I vomit in the kitchen sink. I shave every last trace of hair on my head and face as fast as I can. I take two shirts, three sets of underwear, two pairs of socks, whatever money I can find, my camera, my laptop, one last look at my room, and I leave. I lock the door, slip the key back into the house through the slats in the window, my heart thudding, and I turn around and I start walking again. My heart calms down.

As long as I don't stop walking, my heart stays calm.

3. Pradip

Bhenchod! What was that sound?

I swing the huge searchlight around. The beam is a long, solid lathi of light. The darkness scurries from it as if the lathi is coming to beat it to death.

Nothing.

Thank god.

I mop a thick film of sweat from my forehead. Nothing.

I release the catch in my breath.

One of these nights, saala, it's going to be something.

And I'm going to be its first target.

Along with this big, *saandd-chod* of a searchlight.

Three days back after the in-charge sahab told me I had watchtower duty for the next four nights, he asked me if I wanted to make a phone call to my wife. I had said, 'No, sahab, don't worry, I'll come down alive.' And I had laughed nervously as if it were a bad joke. The sahab had looked at me as if I didn't know what I was talking about.

I didn't.

How the hell was I to know? I have a son, bhai. Next month, he'll be two. I want to see him in a school. How was I to know this is what schools have become these days? Barracks in the classrooms. Briefings in the library. Writing desks for sandbags. Target practice on chalk circles on blackboards. Barbed wire along the compound walls. And this – watchtower – where morning assembly should be. Bhenchod! What was that?

I swing the light around again. This time I let the beam glide slowly through the darkness, peering hard for any movement. The light catches parts of trees. The trees stand like soldiers in surrender, their branches held up like broken hands. Maadarchod trees! I should ask the sahab if we can chop them all down. It'll help the sentry see farther.

The trees scare me. There could be a Maoist hiding behind each one. The adivasis say the spirits of the dead collect in the trees. Chutiya saala, shut up, don't . . . don't think such thoughts. Ghosts are fiction. Ram is fact. Hey Ram. Please don't let me die. I'll donate 501 rupees to the temple when I go to Ayodhya. Swear on my mother.

We have to cut these trees down. Again! Something moved there!

I forget to breathe for another minute. My bowels start to tremble. I'm losing count of how many times this has happened by now. *Aren't you scared of this light? Haan?* I swing the beam around like a sword. *This … this … this light, haan? Take this … maadarchod … hiding in the shadows, aren't you afraid?* I hope if I slash at the darkness this way it will make those gutless shadows scurry for cover.

Where do shadows hide?

In more darkness?

Maybe I should just fire one round into those trees. Scare away anyone who might be there.

No! Are you mad? You'll lose your job! If the others think you're scared they'll never take you on a combing operation. It takes one coward to get the whole convoy killed.

But what if I die right now?

Right here.

While the others sleep … or masturbate … or chew paan masala … or write letters to their wives …

… or piss.

I can't even get down from here to go piss until the 5 a.m. relief comes. Bhenchod! I'm like tiger-bait up here. The only big spot of light in one hundred square kilometres of pitch darkness. Sometimes I wonder if the CRPF would even need to be here if the Indian government had given electricity to this part of Malkangiri.

This is so stupid.

All the Maoists have to do to find this camp is to home in on this light like moths to a bulb. I should ask the sahab about this tomorrow. If someone fires a grenade at this light right now …

How will my wife recognize me from the small bits of my body?

How will she cremate me?

Something moved there …

Will she even know?

Looks like a face!

Or will she keep waiting to hear from me?

Should I raise an alarm?

Will anyone know?

Abbe chutiye, of course they will. They will look for you to man the watchtower tomorrow. And they won't be able to find you. Because – shut up shut up! Enough!

It's just that bhenchod tree!

I put my hand on my heart. It beats so loud I worry someone might hear it in this graveyard silence. Its pounding slowly starts to amplify in my ears. Could it be the heartbeat of that tree? Has it moved closer to me?

I'm scared of even going to bed in the morning. I keep having that dream … of being killed by a tree. Those branches throttling my neck. Vines squeezing around me like snakes, crushing – *oh Ram-Ram-Ram-Ram, please protect me.*

The first thing I do when dawn breaks is clamber down the tower, run to that tree and take a long piss on its bark. I watch the dark yellow liquid stain its body, and hope it feels like killing me for it, when I hear sahab's voice from behind me, 'Combing operation for you tonight, Pradip. Get some sleep.'

'Finally,' I say, turning around, 'a chance to kill somebody!' And I laugh nervously as if it were a bad joke. The sahab looks at me as if I don't know what I am talking about.

4. Sushil

'Yeh...' Bapu says, '... jameen,' and watches me paint the words on the big chart paper. 'Humaa-aari,' he pulls the word in the middle like our headmaster does in spelling-dictation class. 'Slow down Bapu, I can't write the words so large so fast,' I say and I write 'jameen' over the 'jameen' once more so it looks thick. So thick, it looks as if Bapu is shouting it out! I laugh. Bapu asks me, 'What's so funny?' I say, 'You are!' and I dip the brush in the katora of black paint. I want to paint a moochhi on top of Bapu's mouth right now. But he's staring at the chart paper. So serious he looks. I start the 'humaari'. 'Why don't we paint this sign in English?' I ask. 'I wonder if those babus can read Hindi.'

'They better,' says Bapu, sounding even more serious, 'it's our national language. They are Indians, the same as us.'

'Then why do they want our land?' I ask, confused, 'don't they have their own?'

'. . . hai,' says Bapu, pointing at the chart paper, 'make sure the last word fits properly.'

I sit under an imli tree and watch Bapu. He is standing in the sun holding the chart paper across his chest. It looks like a shield. A magic protection. Like Karan had in the Mahabharat. I should have painted that moochhi below his nose. He would have looked like a warrior. All the farmers of Bijapur have collected now. All? No. Where's Nagesh's bapu? Oh, even Ramesh's bapu is not here. But there's Sodi's bapu. And Kalmu's. But Javed's? He promised Bapu he'd be here!

Wait, let me count.

1, 2, 3, 4, 5, 6, 7, 8 …

Twenty-three! Only twenty-three bapus? How will only twenty-three bapus save our fields from the factory babus?

A big car has parked itself near the 'Venus Steel' board. Nobody is getting off. Even the windows are closed. They are dark. I can't see inside. There's a truck coming. It's full of policewallahs. How smart they look in that green uniform! I will tell Bapu tonight that I want to be a policewallah when I grow up.

Arre, why are they pointing their guns at our bapus? I run towards them to stop them. They all have Chinese features. With those slit eyes that we make when we pull at the corners of our eyes with our fingers. Are they from China? Why are they in Indian uniform? *I* should be in that uniform, not *them*.

I shout at them. I tell them that that man with the magic shield is my Bapu. That I painted those words on my Bapu's magic shield. That they are in Hindi, our national language. That, when translated in English, they mean: 'This … land … is … ours.'

One of them pushes me to the side. His hand is so strong I get scared. I stand quietly. I see them gather everyone like I used to gather the goats for grazing. They put all the bapus into the truck. Bapu looks at me from there. He looks so helpless. I think he's also scared.

But the policewallahs don't look scared. The policewallahs never look scared. Everyone listens to the policewallah.

Maybe, if I become a policewallah, no one will ever be able to take my land away from me.

5. Lohhovalsa

While Sushil had his gun trained on this nervous group of villagers, trying to threaten them into calmness, hoping they'd get scared and volunteer some information, any information, Pradip hit Ghenua one more time. And just when Ghenua was about to retaliate, the young woman, Vaano, threw herself between them. In that one moment, one of the men was pulled back from the brink of certain death. But that didn't save the village from the mayhem to follow.

Vaano's saree slipped off her shoulder, baring her breasts. Pradip's searching eyes fell on them. Vaano shut hers.

As they reached the river at the foot of the hill, Sushil was feeling broken. He had tried to stop Pradip. But then a tribal elder had aimed an arrow at Pradip, and scared, Sushil had helplessly felt his arms raise his rifle and his finger pull the trigger, and he had watched in horror as the man from that tribal museum fell to the ground, a hole in the side of his head spilling blood. Pradip had looked at Sushil, and then he had turned back to Vaano and continued to rape her. Four other jawans strained to keep Ghenua on the ground, as he writhed and grunted and spat like a ferocious jungle cat.

And then they had heard a strange whir and a dull click.

Ranjan caught Kabir taking pictures. In that one moment of deathly silence, the young journalist's presence was exposed. Kabir was now their ticket out. Instantly labelled an urban Maoist sympathizer, he would get the unit not just a reprieve for any suspected transgression, but even a pat on the back.

His raw shoulder hurting with the weight of the sack of *salfi* it now bore, Sushil paused, and hesitantly looked back one last time. Behind them, high up on the hill, the village still shimmered, still being licked by a tongue of fire. Only this time, the fire rose so high it seemed to be teasing the heavens with the tip of its tongue. Climbing up the thick rope of smoke, rose a young child's wail – frail but piercing – higher and higher, up into the dark sky … where tonight no moon dared emerge.

6. Sarkaar

The night after, the full moon is staring white again. The sky's singular bewildered eye. We have just left Lohhovalsa. It's sitting pretty on enough bauxite to make Venus Steel a Fortune 500 company. When Singanna, the head of the Adivasi Sangh in the village, had asked us what we had come here for, Kothari had looked at him blankly and said, 'Development.'

The label on the plastic mineral water bottle I had been carrying was pink. The young adivasi man Ghenua had never seen a plastic bottle before. He asked if he could keep it. He could carry drinking water in it into the fields with him every day. I hadn't expected to be the one who'd bring plastic into his life. But, I consoled myself, it was just a matter of time before someone did.

He particularly liked the shade of pink.

7. Vaano

Puvala says these walls are fun. They crumble to dust when he hits them with his tiny fist. It makes him feel strong, he tells me. Like that flying god the Hindu priest had come and drawn outside Baba's hut. Hanuman, he had called it. The pondit had told us that that monkey god can take away all our troubles. But I also remember him telling us a story. Of when that god had set fire to a city with his tail.

A city with walls.

These walls are otherwise so hard. I remember the day Balema's bull had gone mad. It had come charging at our hut. All he had made in that wall was a little crack. But now Puvala looks tired. After all, how many burnt walls can a little boy smash?

I hold my half-burnt saree up to see if I can use it again. He pokes his head through the hole. I never felt like covering my breasts before. I don't know why I feel ashamed of them now. Puvala twists his head around in the hole in my saree, and grins at me. With my teeth I tear the blackened *aanchol* off. Puvala is jumpy. He tugs at my elbow. I lift a burnt mud plate off a basket, slip my hand inside and take out a butterfly. I am holding its wings pinned between my first finger and thumb. Puvala's eyes light up like fireflies. I tie the butterfly's body with a thread and hold it up for him. It tries to escape, flapping its wings hard. Puvala loves this fluttering toy. Its wings are dark red in colour. Like the dirty blood that comes out of me every new moon.

The blood was due this morning. It's never late. Something's wrong.

Is that why I feel ashamed?

Puvala swings the red butterfly around in circles. The butterfly flaps a few more times. Then it just dangles.

Till it dies.

Puvala spots another butterfly nearby. He drops this toy and chases it. The new butterfly settles on a rock. Puvala creeps up behind it very slowly. He tries to catch it, but the butterfly escapes. Puvala runs after it for a long time, trying to catch it. But it flutters out of his hands every time.

The sun has started to set.

I turn back to my saree. It is torn almost in two, burnt black around the edges. I hold it up against the sun, to look at it properly. It looks like a large, dead butterfly. A butterfly that I must have chased and caught. A pink butterfly. *The colour of the insides of ...*

Puvala comes running back. He is panting. He stops near his butterfly-on-a-string. It lies on the ground where he had dropped it. It is now covered in ash. Just like all of us. He picks it up and swings it around. 'This dead butterfly is more fun,' he says to me. 'It will do whatever I want it to.'

Just like the burnt walls, I think.

Puvala starts spinning the dead butterfly in circles over his head. He tells me he feels strong again. 'Just like Hanuman.'

8. Three Naught Three

Constable Channu's mother and father were adivasi. That's a strange thing to say, he knows, but he chose to convert. He goes to the Hanuman temple every week. Only his mother ever calls him Channu any more. He chose for himself a name that makes light of his situation ... Manoranjan. 'Entertainment', he explains, to anyone who asks what his name means. 'So much blood flows in these parts', he adds, 'I thought the region could do with some Manoranjan.' And he laughs. Up until today, everyone always saw the joke.

This boy didn't. He threw Manoranjan a strange look. A

look that seemed to say that the joke was *on* him. Manoranjan remembers this look from somewhere, he just can't remember where. It unsettles him. It makes him feel naked, as if this boy can see right through his vardi, his skin, his flesh and blood, into his soul. He'll have to be careful what he says to this boy, he thinks. What was his name again?

'Kabir,' says Kabir, pointing at himself, and then through the bars of his jail cell, he points at the four young men in the cell across from his, and gestures 'who?'

One of the four adivasi men smiles back at Kabir and calls out their names, pointing them out as he does, 'Mandingi ... Himrika ... Tama,' and he points at himself, 'Bala.'

'What did they do?' Kabir asks Manoranjan. 'Hmph ... Ask me what did they *not* do,' says the constable, dropping machine oil into a rifle's joints. 'Unlawful assembly,' says Bala. Kabir looks at him, surprised. 'Armed,' finishes Bala, 'yes, I speak English.'

Manoranjan cuts in, 'Don't bother knowing, boy, you're off tomorrow to whatever city you got soft in. This kind of information gives your kind of people sleepless nights.'

'We were protesting the illegal detention of some twelve-year-old boys from our village,' says Bala.

'Kids?' Kabir exclaims, 'what were they arrested for?'

'Waging war against the state,' says Bala, and smiles sadly. Mandingi wants to know what they are talking about. Bala, it appears, tells him exactly what he just told Kabir. The sad smile spreads to all the other faces like a mini epidemic. Kabir feels himself smiling too. A resigned smile. One that lifts the ends of his lips in a silent, non-violent revolt against hopelessness. 'They were carrying their bows and arrows,' finishes Bala.

'They smashed my camera,' says Kabir to Bala, and waits for him to finish translating it for his brothers, before adding, 'with their big heavy boots.'

Manoranjan is still listening in, starting to enjoy this conversation, but not letting on that he is, when Kabir is asked which gaon he's from. Kabir tells them about his 'village' – Mumbai … the terror attack nearly a year back … his dead friend … how he started walking … and never stopped … and how he can never return to live in a city ever again.

'You will, boy, you most certainly will,' Manoranjan mutters to the fourth 303 rifle of the night.

Himrika is in tears. He is shocked at all that Kabir's 'village' had to go through. 'How could they?' he asks Bala, 'how could they kill so many people with guns?' The thought of it makes the three tribal men come into a huddle, their voices quivering with the imagined horror.

'Tama is asking how come after the hell you went through, you decided to come here? And help us?' asks Bala. Manoranjan, curious, sneaks a look at Kabir from the corner of his eye.

'*I* went through!' exclaims Kabir, 'Man, I went through nothing compared to what you go through every day. Ten men came into my city. *Ten*. And nine of them got killed for what they did. Here there are thousands of men barging into your homes, robbing you of your food and chickens, raping you, setting your fields on fire, throwing you in jail simply for being what you are, and you think *I* went through hell! Tama, *this* is hell, not where I come from.'

Bala has to control his sides from splitting when he translates that for his brothers. When he's done, the four of them laugh till their eyes burst.

'I'm glad you can see the funny side,' mutters Kabir to himself, a little rattled by the reaction.

'*Manoranjan*,' announces Manoranjan smugly, 'it's what keeps us from slitting our own throats. I told you.'

Kabir notices now what Manoranjan has been doing all this while. 'You know the 26/11 attackers had these fancy automatic rifles,' he says. Manoranjan doesn't respond. His head lowered, he keeps cleaning the rifle barrel with a jhadoo stick. 'You know what the Mumbai police had to fight them with?' asks Kabir.

'Three naught threes,' says Manoranjan, without looking up.

'Can you imagine?' asks Kabir.

'Can *I* imagine?' Manoranjan snaps, 'Can *I* imagine? Of course I can imagine you stupid son-of-a-city! You know why we normal policewallahs don't stand a chance against the Mao-vaadis? Because they have grenade launchers, AK-47s, bazookas and RDX. And we have this – this big elephant dick. It takes five seconds to reload. In that much time you can finish off an entire truck of policewallahs with a single AK-47. So? So we don't risk it. We stay put in our thanas, hoping the Mao-vaadis won't get bored and come bomb us here. And what does the centre do? No, they don't send us new guns. They send us machine oil, heaps of it! So much oil that I can bathe in it every morning. And they ask us, in their official circulars, to clean and service our 303s. Failing which, they send in the CRPF. Central Reserve Police Fucks! Maadarchods who use their cocks more than their bandooks.'

Kabir and Bala exchange a look. Mandingi, perplexed, asks what the policewallah is saying so excitedly. Bala gestures for him to wait, the policewallah is far from finished.

Manoranjan snaps a 303 shut with such force that a spring flies out of it, bounces off a wall, leaps about the floor and rolls to a stop near Kabir's foot. Kabir goes down on his haunches, reaches his hand out through the bars of his jail cell and picks it up. He holds it out for Manoranjan to come pluck it from his fingers. But Manoranjan simply gestures to throw it towards him. Kabir throws. The spring does land in Manoranjan's wide flat hand but it promptly bounces right out of it and flies out of the door. 'Ever heard of *adjustment*?' asks Manoranjan. Kabir quietly shakes his head. This is a speech he doesn't want to interrupt.

'You Mumbai people do it all your lives,' continues Manoranjan, scrubbing the rifle's rusty steel barrel with stale toothpaste. 'You adjust with the babus ... the builders adjust with the police ... the underworld adjusts with the law and order system ... isn't that how you survive there? Don't tell me you've never bribed a traffic havaldar when you jumped a light?' he looks at Kabir in an open challenge. 'I have,' says Kabir. 'We have too,' says the constable, 'we have sometimes bribed the Mao-vaadis to not attack us. To let us live. To let even those adivasis live who have chosen to surrender to the system. We're all human, bhai. None of us want to die. And then these CRPF *lunds* walk in like Mumbai film heroes and talk of a 'war' with the jungle-bhai. Abbe?! Is this Kargil, that we need a war to solve things? And what happens in the process? You idiots end up in jail cells. And I – another idiot – have to spend a sleepless night guarding you when I could've been happily drunk or fucking my wife at home.'

Manoranjan's brain freezes.

'Fucking-my-wife,' he repeats inside his head.

'Fucking'

'My'

'Wife.'

And he looks up at Kabir. The same look has returned in the boy's eyes. *'That's* it,' thinks Manoranjan, *'that* is the look she used to give me. That look of pity. Pity, because I was stuck in a posting in that far-off Maoist hotbed, that *jhaantt* of a place. Pity, because when I had come home after fifteen months I had asked her to get the khatiya out, and though she had waited ten minutes, I had not been able to get it up. Pity, because I finally had my request for a transfer approved, and come back home, just in time to see Malkangiri become a Maoist hotbed too. Pity, because now, any night I'm home, and we choose the khatiya over the chataai, I still can't get it up. And Sundari looks at me with this – *this* look. As if I need to cry my heart out, and be put to sleep. Not fucked, like every other hot-blooded man needs to be.'

'Pity.'

'This boy, he knows something,' thinks Manoranjan, his brain slowly thawing back to normal, 'the way he looks at me, the *lund*.' And as Manoranjan continues to speak to himself, his ears flush bright red, 'On some other night, boy, I would have shown you what it costs to look at a policewallah that way. But not tonight, can't do much damage to you if I can't even get it up now, can I?' And before he realizes it, Manoranjan is laughing. Hard. It unsettles him to hear himself laugh this way, his body convulsing. But he notes that it unsettles the city boy too. So just for that, he keeps on laughing.

While Kabir continues to look at him that way.

9. Ghenua

I used to get drunk and daydream. My back would turn into my bow. My fingers would be arrows. I would point my finger at the deer.

I would bend my back till I could bend it no more. Then I would release it. PTTAANNGG! My finger would shoot out of my fist.

I will never drink any more.

The jungle-bhais have taken my bow away. They put this thing in my hands. They call it a 'bandhuka'. It's so heavy. Like Baba's dead body. The mouth of the gun is a round hole. This is where that hot, hard metal thing must have come flying out from. The thing that made the hole in Baba's head.

I'll do it to that police-lok. His head won't have a hole in it. It will split open. And then I will wear that hot, hard metal thing around my neck.

When those two men came in their big gaadi last year, the younger one had said there was metal in the earth under our village. Is this what they make out of the metal? These hot, hard things that make holes in heads?

Singanna is looking at me. He has no pity in his eyes. I like that. I also don't want any pity in mine. Not when I am face-to-face with that police-lok again.

The jungle-bhais make me make promises. I make them. I will make any promise. I will wear any vardi. I will do anything. Not sleep. Not eat meat. Not drink. Not enter a woman. Now I can never fill her womb with my child.

That makes my eyes wet.

I can't let my eyes ever get wet again.

I look up at my sal tree far away, near the village. Even from here I can see the *motka* tied near the top. Even from here I can smell the sap oozing out from the cut in the bark and collecting in the motka.

Even from here, I can hear myself scream as they struggled to hold me down. Four of them.

Weaklings.

I don't need this 'bandhuka'. Those police-lok do.

All I need is this – this forest. Will this forest ever be ours again?

Every time I have these thoughts, my eyes get wet. If I drink a gourd-ful of *salfi* right now this feeling will go away. But then I look at Singanna. And my eyes don't feel like getting wet any more.

A tall man asks me if I'll kill for the jungle. His voice has the deep hum of the roots of a tree. I tell him that one day I killed a deer with my arrow. When I cut it open, I found a foetus inside. I threw it to the dog.

10. Eyu Kolo

It was evening before the officer-in-charge finally suggested they get water from the adjoining village. He asked for volunteers. Ten seconds passed like jaggery melting.

Thick.

Slow.

Sticky.

Sticking to each man's breath and hardening there in a messy embroidery.

The adjoining village was an adivasi village too. Like every other village in the area. All these villages had heard of what had happened at Lohhovalsa the night before. Adivasis everywhere were now scared.

And a scared beast is a dangerous thing.

No one knew that better than Pradip. He was looking at the searchlight now, its large eye shut, as if it were sleeping. He muttered a prayer to the OC inside his head. He asked him for watchtower duty again if need be. But not this.

'Pradip!' the OC barked, sharp at the dot of the tenth second, 'Sushil! Two jerry cans each. They should last us till morning. Hopefully the supply truck will arrive tomorrow.'

Sushil's heart began to drum again. His eyes had been wide with apprehension. Now as he felt his eyelids grow heavy, he felt his feet move by themselves. Even as he drew in a long, deep breath, he found that two large plastic jerry cans had ballooned in his fists and he was walking out of the school gates.

School.

'I have to start calling it a CRPF camp', he muttered to himself, as his feet picked up a quicker rhythm. 'What?' asked Pradip, thinking he had been spoken to. Sushil simply looked at him and walked faster. The boots made a lot of noise as they fell on the gravel like rubber hammers. It was as if these boots had been made to trample over lives. 'Quite perfect,' thought Sushil, 'I hate them.' And he saw that Pradip had started to jog. 'Don't slow us down. I want to be back in camp by sunset,' he called out, 'don't want to get raped by an adivasi now, do you?'

Sushil drew in another long, deep breath, and slowed down.

He had to stop once to ask an old adivasi woman where the village '*eyu kolo*' was. She looked at him grimly and said something. Sushil didn't understand one word. He looked at her hands, hoping she'd point him in some direction. She didn't. She simply kept talking at him, sounding angrier and angrier, a hundred wrinkles on her face changing shape every second until her skin resembled a map to some secret place where Sushil ought to be right now instead of here.

He turned from her and kept walking, trying to figure where the centre of the village might be. That's where the tube well would have to be too.

When he finally found it, he had walked past dozens of suspicious eyes watching him go by in a rustling silence. He had simply followed the thickening of the groups, hoping that where they clustered most would be where their water sprang from. And he had heard the creaking of the pump handle even before he turned the corner. Pradip was already there, halfway through one can, pumping the lever, possessed. He had his eyes lowered, trained on the fast-filling can, so he could shut out all the eyes that stared at him strangely from all around him.

Sushil put his cans down and told Pradip to 'slow down, we don't want to make them nervous'. Sushil turned to run his eyes over the gathering mob, trying to muster a weak smile at them. The creaking of the pump abruptly stopped. He saw Pradip sitting down on a rock, his chest heaving, still looking at the ground before him. Pradip simply said, 'You pump then.'

Sushil felt his blood rise up into his face as a dam inside him cracked a leak. 'What? Why? You fill yours, I'll fill mine. Now get to it.'

'I can't do it slowly. If it makes them nervous, too bad. If you've got a problem with that, you pump,' said Pradip, glowering at Sushil, and then quickly darting his eyes around to check just how many they had now been surrounded by. Sushil could smell the fear on his colleague. It made the blood in him rise up even further. A red tidal wave slammed into the dam inside his head.

'Bhenchod,' he said, 'we're shitting bricks because of what *you* did; now get up and pump. We don't have time.'

'What!' snapped Pradip, his body growing taut, 'What did you say? What *I* did?' and he charged Sushil like a dog whose tail had been trod upon. 'What *I* did? Suddenly you're one of *them* now? Just because we're surrounded by them? Girgit saala, changing your colours?!'

'Calm down, you fool,' Sushil hissed, looking around at the mob. He thought he heard some titters. And that made him go cold. 'Don't lose your head again.' Before Sushil could turn to look at Pradip again, the half-full jerry can crashed into his face.

The red tidal wave burst from his nose.

The sun had started to set when Sushil finally took his hands off his face. He didn't know how long he had been sitting there tasting the blood and tears as they trickled in through the ends of his mouth and dissolved in his saliva. His hands had finally stopped trembling now. He lowered them, so he could see what he had done.

Pradip lay face down near the tube well, a large smudge of blood clotting in the mud around him. His head was obscured by a large rock. It was the one he had sat down on. Through his tears Sushil saw the crowd gathered there. They were one big blur to him. The rising murmur of their collective voices was one big blur too. So was the corpse, its thick ugly boots going out of focus even as he stared at them. Everything was hazy now.

What was he doing here?

Where was he supposed to be?

He did not know.

It quickly became darker. From somewhere beyond the trees, a bright fat beam of light sprung out at him. It started sweeping through the twilight this way and that, cleaning out any confused shadows that still lingered in its path. Sushil stared at the light.

It seemed to surgically cut through the blur in his vision. He staggered to his feet. With a trembling hand he pumped some water out, splashed it on his face.

His face still dripping, he walked towards the mob of adivasi villagers, waded through them, watching the swollen body of jungle people part as he approached, letting him through. Everything was still a blur, except for that light. He knew where it came from. And looking back over his shoulder, he walked away from it, his tears drying faster the further away he went.

11. Lohhovalsa

He had made her wear it for him. She had crushed a thousand berries and vegetables trying to get the right shade of dye. The saree now looked just like his plastic bottle. Pink.

The women and men had danced in a long line, curving around the fire like a human snake. They had sung about a happy life. A life of harmony. Between hill and river. Between sky and land. Fire and rain. Sun and moon. The boat and the river. Between tree and beast. Bird and flower. Now and the past. And the future.

Switching rhythms, he had tripped through the dancing snake. Sliding past her, Ghenua had whispered in her ear that this pink was the colour of the insides of his Vaano's flower.

And in that moment the colour had spilled out onto her cheeks too.

And just as Baba beat the drum to proclaim them husband and wife, there had been a gunshot. Followed by shouts, the sounds of pots being broken, frightened livestock and bamboo doors being kicked in.

Epilogue

Kabir

A CRPF soldier sits on a milestone by the roadside. His shoes are a dark bottle green. He glares at our passing bike. The automatic rifle thrown lazily across his left shoulder shifts to the right as his head turns to inspect our faces. The milestone below him reads '65 km'. The name of the town is hidden by green camouflage print.

It could be the town we're leaving behind.

It could be the one he's headed to.

It could be where the police fired on a crowd of unarmed adivasis who were protesting the wrongful arrests of their men and children, killing a few on the spot.

It could be where several villages were burnt to the ground to teach the adivasis a 'lesson' for sympathizing with the Maoists.

It could be where the Maoists tied a policeman to an eighty-year-old tamarind tree, beat him to death and set fire to it.

It could be the town where the lower castes and the adivasis clashed over the ownership of the lands they till, where homes were destroyed and two boys hacked.

It could be the town with the board that announces a new mining project by a multinational company on the adjoining adivasi land.

It could be a town that used to be an adivasi village. Where the 'naked' tribals were hounded out, and the educated were housed in brick homes.

Or it could be a town that used to be a fragrant dense grove of mango trees. One of which was a tribal deity, and is the only one that remains.

It could be where we would have died to live.

It could be where we were warned not to go.

It could be north of the border, in Orissa.

Or it could be south of the border, in Andhra Pradesh.

It could be anything.

It could be anywhere.

And it would always be sixty-five kilometres too far.

Jealously guarded by those it housed.

Coveted by those that needed it.

Forgotten by those who passed through.

Called different names by them all. At different times in history.

Born in blood.

To die in blood.

But to belong to no one. Its name obscured by a patch of green camouflage print.

(28 November 2009, from a byline rejected by the newspapers)

'Butterflies on Strings' was inspired by the writings, photographs and experiences of Javed Iqbal, and the relentless good work of Sharanya Nayak.

'Losing too is still ours; and even forgetting still has a shape in the kingdom of transformation.
When something's let go of, it circles; and though we are rarely the center of the circle, it draws around us its unbroken, marvelous curve.'

—Rainer Maria Rilke

WHERE SOME OF THESE STORIES FIRST APPEARED

- 'By/Two' in *Mumbai Noir* edited by Altaf Tyrewala, in 2012
- 'Red, 17' in *Eid Stories*, in 2010; and *Saleem on Earth and other stories*, in 2013
- 'The Fag End' in *Penguin First Proof* 7, in 2012
- 'A River of Cotton' and 'Butterflies on Strings' in slightly different form in *Emanations*, edited by Carter Kaplan, in 2011
- 'Carborised', 'Equestrian', 'Untreated', 'Forest Fire', 'Breach', 'Ambush', 'Mine', 'The Apology', 'Bindi', 'The First Bite' in slightly different form in *Terribly Tiny Tales*, edited by Anuj Gosalia, in 2013-14
- 'Disengaged', 'Going Home', 'Letting Go', 'Occupying Silence', 'Jugalbandi', 'Still Life', 'Load-shedding', 'Refugee', 'The Race', 'The Test', 'The Initiation' and 'Beautiful People' in slightly different form in *Occupying Silence*, in 2008

ACKNOWLEDGEMENTS

Raghunath Makhija
Bharati Makhija
Simiran Makhija
Jyoti Dogra
Sugandha Garg
Sharanya Rajgopal
Aradhna Singh
Kavita Rayirath
Rohini Das
Rashika Pratap Singh
Faiza Ahmad Khan
Ishita Moitra
Priyanka Raja
Pravishi Das
Chatura Rao
Archana Menon
Neel Dasgupta
Abhijeet Chakravarty
Priya Darshini
Gayatri Patel

Rajat Nagpal
Karan Makhija
Dr Rraajnath Chakravarty
Dr Fayaz Alam
Dr K.K. Sengupta
Philo Joseph
Dhanu Kandappah
Mita Kapur
Jaideep Sahni
Abbas Tyrewala
Anurag Kashyap
Sneha Khanwalkar
Amit Sharma
Salim bhai
Vitasta Raina
Bivashkumar Ganguli
Jaya Stores
Don Bosco, Park Circus

My gratitude, and apologies, to all those others whose lives I might have unwittingly stolen from. Being a storyteller, that's an occupational hazard I can do nothing to remedy. Hopefully, I've used the raw material to your unwitting satisfaction.

And lastly, a big thank you to Death, my most precious teacher. If I wasn't this familiar with Her, the little life I've lived wouldn't seem worth cherishing.

ABOUT THE AUTHOR

Devashish Makhija has written and directed the full-length award-winning feature films *Joram*, *Bhonsle* and *Ajji*, all three of which screened at numerous international film festivals, winning awards widely; and the multiple-award-winning short films *Cycle*, *Cheepatakadumpa*, *Taandav*, *El'ayichi*, *Agli Baar*, *Rahim Murge pe Mat ro*, *Absent* and *Happy*.

Bhonsle (winner of a National Award in 2021) is streaming on Sony Liv. *Joram* (winner of two Filmfare Awards in 2024) and *Ajji* are on Amazon Prime Video.

Makhija is a multi-practice artist. He has had his own solo art show 'Occupying Silence' and is a prolific writer, having written the bestselling children's books *When Ali became Bajrangbali*, *Why Paploo was Perplexed*, *We are The Dancing Forest*, and the multiple-award-winning YA novel *Oonga*.

HarperCollins *Publishers* India

At HarperCollins India, we believe in telling the best stories and finding the widest readership for our books in every format possible. We started publishing in 1992; a great deal has changed since then, but what has remained constant is the passion with which our authors write their books, the love with which readers receive them, and the sheer joy and excitement that we as publishers feel in being a part of the publishing process.

Over the years, we've had the pleasure of publishing some of the finest writing from the subcontinent and around the world, including several award-winning titles and some of the biggest bestsellers in India's publishing history. But nothing has meant more to us than the fact that millions of people have read the books we published, and that somewhere, a book of ours might have made a difference.

As we look to the future, we go back to that one word—a word which has been a driving force for us all these years.

Read.

Harper Collins

4th

HARPER PERENNIAL

HARPER BUSINESS

HARPER BLACK

हार्पर हिन्दी

HarperCollins *Children'sBooks*

HARPER DESIGN

HARPER VANTAGE

Harper Sport